HE CAME AROUND ONE OF THE TABLES AND SAW IT. A STEAMING PILE OF SOMETHING, CLOTHING AND SKIN AND GENERAL BLOODY ICKINESS. MOST OF IT WAS UNRECOGNIZABLE.

Xander felt nauseated. He put a hand over his nose and mouth, both to block out the smell and to keep himself from getting sick. "Oh my God," he said. "Oh God."

He had to get help. *Buffy and the others are in the library,* he thought. *I could be there in less than a minute, if I leave right now. Especially if I run.*

Running was definitely in the plan.

He turned to do just that, but then he didn't.

Because when he turned, he found himself face-to-face with a monster from his worst nightmares.

Buffy the Vampire Slayer™

Buffy the Vampire Slayer (movie tie-in)
The Harvest
Halloween Rain
Coyote Moon
Night of the Living Rerun
Blooded
Visitors
Unnatural Selection
Power of Persuasion
Deep Water
The Angel Chronicles, Vol. 1
The Angel Chronicles, Vol. 2
The Angel Chronicles, Vol. 3
The Xander Years, Vol. 1
The Xander Years, Vol. 2
The Willow Files, Vol. 1

Available from ARCHWAY Paperbacks and POCKET PULSE

Buffy the Vampire Slayer adult books

Child of the Hunt
Return to Chaos
The Gatekeeper Trilogy
Book 1: Out of the Madhouse
Book 2: Ghost Roads
Book 3: Sons of Entropy
Obsidian Fate
Immortal
Sins of the Father
Resurrecting Ravana
Prime Evil

The Watcher's Guide: The Official Companion to the Hit Show
The Postcards
The Essential Angel
The Sunnydale High Yearbook
Buffy the Vampire Slayer: Pop Quiz

Available from POCKET BOOKS

BUFFY THE VAMPIRE SLAYER™

THE XANDER YEARS

Vol. 2

A Novelization by Jeff Mariotte
Based on the hit TV series created by Joss Whedon
Based on the teleplays "The Pack" by Matt Kiene & Joe Reinkemeyer,
"Go Fish" by David Fury & Elin Hampton, and "The Zeppo"
by Dan Vebber

POCKET PULSE
New York London Toronto Sydney Singapore

This book is a work of fiction. Names, characters, places and incidents are products of the author's imagination or are used fictitiously. Any resemblance to actual events or locales or persons, living or dead, is entirely coincidental.

An *Original* Publication of POCKET BOOKS

POCKET PULSE, published by
Pocket Books, a division of Simon & Schuster Inc.
1230 Avenue of the Americas, New York, NY 10020

ISBN: 0-671-03920-2

First Pocket Pulse printing April 2000

10 9 8 7 6 5 4 3 2 1

Printed in the U.S.A.

This one's for Holly and Amanda, true Xander fans.
And Dave, who's partial to Herbert.

Acknowledgments

It takes a lot of people to write a book. I'd like to thank some of those who helped me with this one. First of all, my friend Chris Golden, who got the ball rolling. Maryelizabeth Hart and Nancy Holder, who held my hands all the way through. Christine, Tigger, Scott, and Denise, for moral support. Lisa Clancy and Micol Ostow, State Champions of the editorial world. Nicholas Brendon, for his perfect portrayal of Xander. And Joss Whedon, without whom . . .

THE XANDER YEARS

Vol. 2

PROLOGUE

There wasn't much traffic—Sunnydale tended to be the kind of town that rolled up its sidewalks and went to bed early—but that didn't mean there was none, and what there was, Xander found. He made a right onto Palm, and a bright red muscle car roared out of nowhere at him, headlights blinding. It swerved around him, jerked back into the lane directly in front of him, and then raced away with a growl and a blast of exhaust.

It shook Xander, but he let it slide off him. Nothing was going to spoil his mood tonight. Besides, he knew he wasn't in any mortal danger. Mostly, he realized, he didn't want to have to deal with the questions the police would ask if there had been an accident. What are you doing out so late? Where are you going? Why doesn't the name on the vehicle's registration match the one on your driver's license?

A brief moment of panic, and then he remembered

that yes, he was carrying his license. He always did—it was just the driving part that was rare.

The name on the license was Alexander Lavelle Harris, but except for his mother when she was angry—and that stretch in fifth grade when he'd gone through his Alexander the Great phase—he was always called Xander. He had always lived right here in Sunnydale, always figured that he'd grow up and grow old hanging with Willow and Jesse and despising Cordelia, and that one day he'd die right here in Sunnydale.

Okay, that day was looking like it might arrive sooner rather than later.

But the key word here was "always."

Life had seemed pretty set, Xander thought. *I knew who I was, where I'd be, what I'd do.* When he tried to see himself in the future he saw basically the same thing he saw in the mirror, only maybe with shorter hair and a tie, or worse yet, one of those cardigan sweaters TV dads wore.

All that was before Buffy Summers had come to Sunnydale.

Blond and beautiful, as fit as you could hope for—Buffy was Xander's ideal of feminine perfection. He'd been taken with her from the moment he'd seen her, and he stayed that way. Every time he saw her was like seeing her fresh again.

He knew now that he'd never be "with" Buffy in the way that he wanted, but standing beside her—*okay, a little behind, and maybe off to the side*—as she faced down evil was just as good in its way. He was part of her inner circle, part of the Scooby Gang, and important to Buffy's life. How did it get better than that?

Buffy had brought all kinds of new things into Xander's life, and sure, some of them, like vampires and witches and giant praying mantises, he could live without. But when one got right down to it, the most significant thing that Buffy brought was change. Status wasn't quite so quo with her around.

Made life exciting, that was for sure.

If you looked at Sunnydale, you wouldn't think anything had changed, but then really—Xander reminded himself—it hadn't. He knew now that Sunnydale had always been situated on a hellmouth. It was his perception of his hometown that was different. The shadows seemed darker, the nights longer, the silences, well, quieter.

He glanced out the passenger side at the Bronze, just where it had always been. But there had been a time when he thought it was just a place to chill with his friends. In those long-gone days before he'd seen people he knew killed there. He still went there to listen to music, drink a mochaccino, hang with Buffy and Willow and Oz and Cordy . . . but every now and then he had a flash of some of the things he'd seen there and got a little tingle up his spine.

Not the kind of tingle he liked, either.

Those times, he felt a touch of sorrow for the loss of innocence that Sunnydale had suffered since Buffy came to town. And then he reminded himself, yet again, that the innocence lost hadn't been the town's. It was his. It was something he'd never have back again.

Yes, he'd changed. No denying it. Xander was still just Xander, to the outside world. But his inner Xander was someone else, someone who couldn't bring himself to eat a hot dog or a ham sandwich anymore. So far, nothing evil had cropped up to interfere with his enjoyment of chocolate, thank God.

But this was Sunnydale. Heinousness perched around

every corner, lurked behind every happy facade. Living here was like going through a door at Disneyland and being greeted with a math test.

Home sweet home.

He cruised the silent streets, feeling no particular hurry to get home, on this night especially. He felt good. If he slept, the charge would be gone when he woke up, and he'd just be plain old Xander again. No. He might be sleepy in school tomorrow, but he was going to stay out for a while. Besides, how often did he get to actually drive a car? Sure beat skateboarding, which, in the old, pre-Buff days, had been his only mode of transport.

Instead of making the turn that would take him to his quiet suburban street, he hung a left. He drove slowly down Revello Drive, but didn't stop in front of Buffy's house. That would make him a stalker or something, and a Slayerette didn't stalk the Slayer. At the end of her block he took another left, then a right, and a few minutes later he passed the Sunnydale Mall. He kept on this course, headed toward the ocean. This way took him past Weatherly Park, and since there was still no traffic he opened her up a little bit. The Natural History Museum and the Sunnydale Zoo flashed past on his right.

The zoo. Destination of a hundred trips with family, friends, and classmates. That place brought back memories.

All of them bad.

Gave a whole different meaning to the word "change." Xander shuddered, gripped the wheel a little more tightly, and drove on.

Chapter 1

Buffy Summers strolled through the Sunnydale Zoo, enjoying the way the sun warmed her cheeks on this cool spring day. She walked alone, intent on the zoo map, comparing points on it to the posted signs. Maybe there was something here they didn't have in Los Angeles. *Although, this being Sunnydale,* she thought, *it would probably be some mythical killer beast, a Kraken or a Wendigo or something.*

"Oh, look."

The familiar voice caught her attention and she looked up. Kyle DuFours. Creepy Kyle, Willow called him sometimes. He came toward her, accompanied by the kids he was always with: Rhonda Kelley, Tor Hauer, and Heidi Barrie. Always together, always annoying. Well, she'd just make a point of avoiding them for the rest of the day. Shouldn't be hard—Kyle's shirt was a yellow so bright she'd be able to spot him from a distance. *Like, say, Kansas.*

"It's Buffy," Kyle said. "And all her friends."

"That's witty," Buffy said. She'd known some kind of obnoxious line was coming. After all, his lips had been starting to move. But she also knew it wasn't over. These guys never let up.

Tor fixed his gaze on her. "Do you ever wonder why nobody cool ever wants to hang out with you?" he asked.

"I'm just thankful," she replied.

"Were you this popular at your old school?" Rhonda asked, getting in on the action. "Before you got kicked out?"

They all resumed walking, almost as one. Rhonda moved past Buffy, nudging her aside with one shoulder. Buffy let it go. *They're just punks,* she thought. *Rude, but harmless.*

"Careful," Tor told Rhonda as he passed Buffy. He stared at Buffy, turning his head as he went by. She wondered, briefly, if he thought he looked cool, or worse, attractive. "She might beat you up."

They all laughed at that knee-slapper, and then they were gone. *Relatively brief and painless,* Buffy thought. *The best kind of encounter to have with them.*

She moved on, stopping to read a display outside the elephant enclosure.

Another voice called out to her. Also familiar, but more friendly. "Hey! Buffy!"

She looked up to see Xander Harris and Willow Rosenberg, her two best friends in the world, running toward her. They looked happy, like they were truly enjoying this little escapade. Maybe they were. They both seemed to have a knack, sometimes, for looking on the bright side.

"You missed it!" Willow said. Enthusiastic. Her usual state of being.

"Missed what?"

"We saw the zebras mating," Xander said. "Thank you, very exciting."

"It looked like the Heimlich. With stripes," Willow added. Her wide smile was usually infectious, but it didn't spread to Buffy this time.

"And I missed it," Buffy said, with mock sadness. "Yet, somehow I'll find the courage to live on."

They started walking, headed nowhere in particular.

"Where were you?" Willow asked her.

"I was looking at the fishes."

"Was it cool?"

Buffy thought about that for a moment. "It was fishes."

"I'm feeling that you're not in the field trip spirit here," Xander said, as if picking up on her decided lack of excitement.

"Well, it . . . it's nothing." She couldn't quite summon the energy to shrug. "Anyway, we did the same zoo trip at my old school every year. Same old, same old."

"Buffy, this is *not* just about looking at a bunch of animals," Xander explained. "This is about *not being in class.*"

This time, Buffy did smile. *He has a point,* she supposed. *Good old Xander, finding the silver lining to every cloud of gloom.* "You know, you're right. Suddenly the animals look shiny and new."

"Gotta have perspective," Xander said.

The chimpanzee enclosure looked like a granite cliff. On a rocky shelf, three chimps—mother, father, and baby—shared lunch. Or, the mother and father did. The young one shrieked and grabbed, but the adults managed to keep their food to themselves.

Lance Lincoln leaned on the rail at the enclosure's edge, spiral notebook open, scribbling down his observations on the chimp family's meal. For him, a field trip wasn't about being away from school, it was about having an opportunity for some good solid insight into primate behavior. He was so involved in his research that he didn't hear the four pairs of footsteps approaching him from behind.

"Lance!"

He turned around. Kyle and his friends, bearing down on him. *Swell,* he thought. *Victim, thy name is Lance.*

"How's it going?" Kyle asked. *Like we're old buddies or something.*

"Hey, Kyle," he replied evenly.

Kyle leaned on the railing next to him, glanced at the chimps. "So this is like a, um, family reunion?"

"No." *Well—from an evolutionary perspective, maybe.* But to go there with Kyle? He didn't think so.

Kyle went on as if Lance hadn't said anything. "I think it's a family reunion. It's so touching. Doesn't anybody have a camera?" He mimicked whipping one out, snapping a picture.

Lance flashed back to grade school, when his love for reruns of the old TV show "Lancelot Link, Secret Chimp" had become common knowledge. Given his name, it would have been hard for him not to be drawn to the show, and it was probably what kick-started his interest in primatology. But the flack he'd taken from schoolmates calling him Lance Link, or Sir Lancelot, had almost driven him away from that calling.

Compared to these bullies, those kids were nothing, he thought.

Rhonda came up behind Lance and started tugging at the hairs on the back of his head. "Hey, does your mom still pick out your lice?" she asked. "Or are you old enough to do that yourself now?"

"Quit it," Lance demanded. He jerked his head away from her.

And in doing so, turned just enough that Tor was able to snatch his notebook from his hand. "Hey! Guys, come on," Lance said, grabbing for the notebook. "I've got all my notes in there!" But Tor held it over his head, out of Lance's reach. Only in the back of his mind, where he catalogued such things, did he vaguely realize that the whole scene duplicated the chimp behavior, with the larger chimps holding food away from the little one.

Terrific. I'm the little monkey, he thought.

The group's laughter was interrupted by the voice of Mr. Flutie, Sunnydale High's principal. "What's going on here?" he asked.

Lance watched him approach. He was no fashion expert, but even he knew Mr. Flutie's plaid sports coat was just wrong. It hung open in front, as if both his belly and his sense of self-importance were too swollen to allow it to button. A shock of dark hair sat atop his head like an afterthought, or a small furry mammal abandoned there by some predator.

"I have had it up to here with you four," Mr. Flutie said. "What are you doing?"

"Nothing," Kyle insisted.

Flutie planted himself in front of Kyle. "Did I ask you to speak? Okay, I guess I did. But I want the truth." He looked at Lance. "Lance?"

Tell the truth—or survive? No real contest. "They weren't doing anything. Really," Lance went along. He even forced a chuckle. "We were just playing around." *Like I'd play around with these guys.*

And yet, Mr. Flutie bought it. "All right." Mr. Flutie started to go, then stopped, swiveled, and raked a finger like a machine gun across the chests of the four trouble-makers. "I'll be watching you," he said, then turned again and headed down the path.

"You," Kyle said, pointing at Lance's face. Lance didn't like the sound of that—or that finger in his eyes. *Now what?* "Came through big time," Kyle went on.

"Way to go, Lance," Rhonda added, patting him on the arm like an old friend.

"Flutie's been looking for a reason to come down on us," Tor said.

Whew. "It's okay," Lance said, trying not to sound too relieved.

Kyle reached out, gripped Lance's collarbone, some-where between a pal and a prison warden. "Come on. We're gonna check out the hyena house."

Lance hesitated. "But—I think it's off limits."

"And therein, my friend, lies the fun."

Lance chuckled again, but to him it sounded even less real than the one he'd given Mr. Flutie. He didn't quite know how to extricate himself—that had been a bonding moment of some kind, he figured, and now they were a unit. He went along.

The pathway to the hyena house was blocked off by yellow caution tape, and signs on easels read "Positively No Admittance." Yet another sign said "Closed." Orange lights flashed on the warning signs. The meaning was pretty clear, Lance figured. The zoo officials didn't want anyone wandering into the hyena exhibit.

Which, according to Kyle, was the "fun part." Lance couldn't quite figure, but he was willing to go along.

After all, they were being nice to him, which was a first. And besides, they had him more or less surrounded. Rhonda lifted the caution tape and they ducked under, headed down the path.

Hyenas, here we come.

Xander, Willow, and Buffy weren't far behind. They saw Lance go under the tape and disappear down the path. There was something very wrong about this picture, and it was as obvious as Lance's bright red sweater—he would never be part of that crowd. Xander knew Lance was no more likely to hang with Kyle and those guys than Willow was. Or himself, even. *Like, not at all.*

"What are Kyle and his buds doing with Lance?" Willow asked.

To Xander, the answer was clear. "Playing with him, as the cat plays with the mouse."

"What is it with those guys?" Buffy asked. They stopped at the tape, looking down the path. Lance and the others were gone from sight.

"They're obnoxious," Willow said. "Professionally."

"Every school has 'em," Xander explained. "You start a school, you get desks, some blackboards, and some mean kids."

Buffy started toward the tape. "Yeah, well, I better extract Lance before—"

But Xander raised a hand to her, stopping her in her tracks. "I'll handle it," he offered. "This job doesn't require actual slaying." *I hope.* He ducked under the tape and headed for the hyenas, fully aware that the two girls behind him were watching him go. A small display of bravery, tiny, really, compared to some of Buffy's. *But, hey—you take what you can get.*

Buffy wasn't convinced. "You don't think we should follow?"

"Kyle and those guys are jerks, but they're all talk." Willow had lived in Sunnydale her whole life and knew the kids better than Buffy. Buffy was inclined to trust her, until Willow added, "Mostly."

"Why don't we—"

Willow agreed with a nod. "Yeah, why don't we—"

They hadn't made it two steps beyond the tape when a zookeeper appeared. "Whoa, hold it, hold it," he said. What hair he had was blond, long in back but mostly dome-like on top. He had a neat blond beard and glasses, an almost professorial demeanor. His voice was gentle, but firm. "Are you blind, or are you just illiterate? Because hyenas are quick to prey on the weak."

"We were just—" Buffy started.

He cut her off mid-sentence. "You're not going in there. Anyone that does is in a world of trouble." He raised the tape for them to slink back out.

Willow, always the peacemaker, chimed in. "No, no one's going in there." She led the way back under the tape.

Buffy wasn't so willing to let it go. "Why is it off limits?" she asked.

"It's a quarantine. These hyenas just came from Africa. So keep out." His voice indicated that he would accept no response other than obedience. But he raised a single eyebrow, giving his face a slightly friendlier aspect. Then he said something that Buffy found very strange. "Even if they call your name."

"What're you talking about?" she asked.

The zookeeper looked even more like a professor as he launched into lecture mode. "A Masai tribesman once told me that hyenas can understand human speech. They follow humans around by day, learning their names." His voice lowered. Now he sounded like a man telling a ghost story. "At night, when the campfire dies, they call out to the person. And once they separate him"—he snapped his fingers—"the pack devours him."

There was more caution tape at the actual entrance to the hyena enclosure. Kyle just ripped it down as he passed through it, so that he was festooned in it for a moment, yellow against his yellow shirt. It was dark in here, shaded, and cooler than outside. The walls were artificial rock, a man-made cave with cutaways for illuminated displays, and a larger one for the hyenas themselves, up a couple of steps, chest-high bars across the front.

Kyle looked around, turning slowly. "Cool."

"I don't see any hyenas," Lance said. He was having second thoughts now. Fifth or sixth thoughts, really. He was ready to go.

Almost as if on cue, a hyena stepped forward from the gloom of its pen, revealing a dark, almost black muzzle, full of large, pointed teeth. It growled. It didn't sound friendly. Now Lance was more than ready to be gone.

"Okay," he said. "Now we've seen it." He turned to go, but Tor was standing right behind him, blocking his way.

And the others hadn't had enough, it seemed. "It looks cute," Rhonda said.

"I think it looks hungry," Kyle said. He stepped away from the bars. He and Tor grabbed Lance, muscled him up the steps toward the cage.

"Come on, Spot!" Tor growled as they dragged Lance

forward. "Suppertime!" They held him in front of the bars—which now seemed considerably shorter and less substantial than they had just a minute ago. The hyena growled again, deep in its throat. Someone had a hand on the back of Lance's head, pushing his face into the cage. Everyone laughed—except Lance.

"Ow!" he complained. "Stop it! That's not funny!"

Xander heard that last part, and had to agree—despite the raucous laughter coming from the Kyle Brigade, none of it sounded terribly humorous. He leapt up the stairs and into the thick of it, yanking people's arms away from Lance. He shoved Lance out of their reach, down the stairs. When Lance was safely away, Xander found himself eyeball to eyeball with Kyle.

"Why don't you pick on someone your own species?" he asked.

Kyle glared back, not giving an inch. "What, are you gonna get in my face?"

The hyena interrupted the stare-down with another long, low growl. It raised its head into the light again, growling more, and then they were all looking at it. The thing was not lovely, but its eyes held a mesmerizing quality, and the five of them found themselves staring into those eyes.

Barely noticing when the eyes flashed with an eerie green glow.

And, of course, they couldn't see their own eyes. Flashing an answering green.

Nor did they, at this moment, notice the bizarre red design painted on the enclosure's floor. The design on which they all stood. Their attention was riveted on the hyena, growling and moving in its cage.

* * *

Lance took advantage of their distraction to make his escape. He started for the exit. Tripped. His notebook slid across the damp floor. He grabbed it up again, hoisted himself to his feet. But the others had heard him fall, were turning—weirdly, turning slowly but in unison—and laughing. Laughing at him, their laughter rising in pitch, becoming almost hysterical.

Xander, who had rescued him, was the last to turn, the only one out of synch, and Lance didn't know what he expected to see on Xander's face but it wasn't what he saw, which was a smile. He wasn't laughing like the others, but the smile—knowing, and without a trace of kindness or real humor—was almost worse.

Lance ran.

Later, Kyle, Rhonda, Tor, and Heidi strolled the zoo grounds. The school buses had long since gone. They had stood in hiding, watching the near-frantic search for themselves, punching each other on the arms and biting back raucous laughter. Finally, Mr. Flutie had given the order to go ahead without them—*Another black mark on our permanent records,* Kyle thought. *Horrors!*

They'd get home somehow. It wasn't that far. Nothing to sweat.

But—and this went unspoken among them—none of them wanted to leave. Something about the place—the sound of hooves scrabbling on dirt, the ruffling of feathers, the sharp smells of feed and fur and filth—drew them. Kept them here.

They felt strangely at home.

They wandered the paths, laughing at the locals looking into the enclosures, and the tourists in from Ohio or Omaha, getting their first glimpse at a real California zoo. An hour or so after the buses had finally gone, they came across a young couple, arm in arm on a bridge, watching ring-tailed lemurs scamper around an island enclosure. The couple looked to be in their late twenties, maybe early thirties. Middle class. He was tall and clean cut, she was smaller, and cute, in that red-haired, freckled way. Young marrieds, intent on starting a family, maybe. Yuppies. Conventional.

Kyle hated them on sight.

He started to say something to the others, but his gaze met Rhonda's and he knew he didn't have to. *We're all on the same page,* he thought.

The couple faced the cage, their backs to the path. Kyle stepped up to the safety railing, next to the redhead.

"Like those monkeys?" he asked her.

"I don't think they're monkeys," she started to say. The man, the husband, just glared at him.

Heidi approached the man, put her hand on his arm as if he were an old friend. A very good friend.

"I think they're funny," she said. "Do you think they can smell us from here?"

"Across the water?" the man asked. "I wouldn't think so." He tugged his arm away, but Heidi persisted.

"You don't mind, do you," she asked the wife. "Donald and I go way back."

"My name's not Donald," he insisted.

"It's not," his wife said, backing him. "It's Henry."

Heidi laughed. "I thought you were going to stop using Henry," she said. "Don't tell me you told her you were a programmer, too."

The man's face was clouding over quickly. "Listen," he grumbled. "I don't know what you're trying to pull here—"

"Oh, very good," Rhonda said. "I'd almost believe it if I didn't know you."

"Henry, you don't know these people, do you?" the redhead asked, almost plaintively.

"Of course not!"

"You're hurting my feelings, Donald," Heidi whimpered. She put her hands on his chest. He brushed them away.

"Be nice, Donald," Tor said. He swelled out his chest and arms, trying to look threatening. "Is that any way to treat old friends?"

The woman's head swiveled like a spectator at a tennis match. Tears started to run down her cheeks.

"I've never seen these people before in my life," Henry thundered. "Now get away from us or I'm calling security!"

"Ooooh," Kyle said in mock terror. "Not that!"

"I mean it." Henry pulled a cell phone from his pants pocket and started to punch in numbers.

"I said, not that!" Kyle slapped Henry's hand from beneath and the tiny phone went flipping end over end, landing with a small splash in the water beneath the bridge.

Henry's face turned bright red. "Do you have any idea how much—"

Kyle cut him off. "Can it, Donald. We're tired of you. You want to lie to this nice lady, pretend you don't know us, that's fine. We don't know you either. Come on, guys."

He started off the bridge, clomping loudly on the wooden crosspieces as he went. He didn't look back, but heard the others following him. Behind them, he could hear Henry and his wife talking, arguing.

Kyle started to laugh. Heidi joined in. Within seconds, they were all laughing so hard they could barely stand. They flopped down on a swatch of grass, rolling with laughter. Loud, high-pitched squeals of laughter, the kind that was so funny that when one of them stopped, the sound of it got him or her going again.

They were still laughing an hour later, when the zoo closed.

CHAPTER 2

The Bronze was crowded—like that was news. When there's only one decent club in town where kids under twenty-one can hear music, drink coffee, dance, and hang out, it's likely to draw a crowd.

Buffy Summers and Willow Rosenberg turned away from the pastry counter. Buffy carried a croissant and a soda. Willow settled for a box of raisins. *She's preoccupied,* Buffy thought. It didn't take a genius to figure out with what. As far as Will was concerned, the sun rose and set with Xander.

She'd felt that way since they were both five years old—a little young for serious romance, but maybe not for a first crush. Even at the time, though, she'd thought it was true love, recognizing that the relationship was not all she hoped for only when Xander broke her Barbie.

Even that, I forgave him, she thought, with a rueful smile. *Even that.*

But in all the years since then, while they'd remained steadfast friends, that was just about as good as she got. Xander, her buddy. Xander, the guy who would complain to her when he was having girl trouble.

Never seeming to realize what he could have had.

"I thought Xander would be here by now," Willow said as they threaded their way toward an open table.

"That'd make him on time," Buffy replied. "We couldn't have that."

"Did he seem at all upset on the bus back from the zoo?"

"About what?"

"I don't know," Willow said. "He was quiet."

Buffy slid onto a seat at one of the chest-high tables. "I didn't notice anything. But then again, I'm not as hyper-aware of him as, oh, say, for example, *you.*"

"Hyper-aware?" Willow asked, taking the stool across from Buffy's.

"Well," Buffy said. "I'm not constantly monitoring his health, his moods, his blood pressure—"

Willow knew that one. "One-thirty over eighty."

Buffy laughed. "You got it bad, girl."

"He makes my head go tingly. You know what I mean?"

"I dimly recall," Buffy said, gaze cast toward the ceiling.

"But it hasn't happened to you lately?"

A shrug. "Not of late."

"Not even for a dangerous and mysterious older man whose leather jacket you're wearing right now?"

Buffy glanced at the jacket Angel had given her. Angel, the tall, dark, mystery hunk whose life kept intersecting with hers in the oddest ways. He had told her that the jacket looked better on her—which wasn't, strictly speaking, even close to true. It was way out of place, for instance, with the pale green dress she was wearing tonight. And yet, she had barely taken it off since he'd given it to her.

"It goes with the shoes," she insisted.

"Come on," Willow said, having none of it. "Angel pushes your buttons. You know he does."

"I suppose some girls might think he's good looking," Buffy relented. "If they . . . have eyes. All right, he's a honey." *Understatement of the month club,* she thought. She didn't want to let on to Willow, though. The poor girl thought the whole situation was terribly romantic, but there was still that Slayer thing to contend with. *Makes dating a little complicated.* "But he's never around, and when he is all he wants to do is talk about vampires, and I just can't have a relationship—"

Willow interrupted with an excited, "There he is!"

Buffy's head swiveled. "Angel?"

"Xander!"

Then Buffy saw him too, wending his way through the crowd, wearing a brown flannel shirt over a dark T. *A little more somber than his usual look,* she thought. And he didn't *move* quite like the Xander Buffy knew—he sauntered, stopping now and again to look at women, smile at women, flirt with women. Okay, so not completely unlike Xander. But he was usually more discreet about it.

Finally, he made his way to their table. "Girls," he said.

"Boy," Buffy replied.

"Sorry I'm late," he went on. "I just forgot we were gonna be here." He looked at Buffy's plate. "Hungry," he said, tearing off a chunk of Buffy's croissant and shoving it into his mouth.

Willow chose to ignore the less-than-polite behavior. She had known Xander since they were five, so Buffy figured that slack-cutting, where he was concerned, was a long-ingrained habit.

"Xander, you still want me to help you with geometry tomorrow?" Willow asked. As she spoke, he downed a swallow of Buffy's drink, without a trace of pleasure. "We can work after class."

"Yeah," he said. Then, indicating Buffy's snack, asked, "What is this crap?"

"Well, it *was* my buttery croissant," Buffy said.

"Man, I need some *food,*" Xander said. His voice carried a tinge of anger, as if she'd ordered the pastry just to offend him. "Birds live on this."

But apparently he wasn't too angry to notice the look that passed between Buffy and Willow. "What?" he asked with an anxious smile.

"What's up with you?" Buffy asked.

Willow took it more personally. She fiddled nervously with her raisin box. "Is something wrong? Did I do something?"

"What could you possibly do?" Xander asked. "That's crazy talk. I'm just restless."

"Well, we could go to the ice cream place . . ." Willow offered.

Xander raised his head, peering over the crowd, as if looking for something. Or just surveying his territory. He scratched his chest. "I like it here."

And as if the way he'd been acting wasn't bizarre enough, he began to sniff Buffy's hair.

"Okay, now what?" she asked.

"You took a bath," he explained. Although "explained" wasn't the word for it, since it didn't actually explain anything. He kept scratching at his shirt. *Fleas?* Buffy wondered.

"Yeah, I often do. I'm actually known for it."

"That's okay," Xander said.

Gee, thanks. Glad I have your blessing. Slipping into announcer-speak, Buffy said, "And the weird behavior award goes to . . ."

But he wasn't even listening anymore. His attention had become riveted on the door. Buffy turned to see what he was so intent on.

And was instantly sorry she had.

Kyle, Heidi, Tor, and Rhonda. *The good-time gang.*

"Oh, great," she said. "It's the winged monkeys."

They walked through the Bronze, making a beeline for the table where Xander stood between Willow and Buffy. Xander couldn't look away, couldn't blink, and was only somewhat aware of that fact. His eyes had locked with Kyle's the moment he came through the door, and they stayed locked. Xander and Kyle had never been friends, but now they shared something.

Xander wasn't sure what it was.

But something, definitely.

They reached Buffy and Willow's table, each of them looking only at Xander. He acknowledged them wordlessly as they went by, and turned to keep them in sight as they passed.

They stopped at a nearby table—one that was already occupied by a couple of kids. One was a stocky guy in a plaid shirt, the other thinner and familiar-looking, though Xander couldn't place him. Kyle and Rhonda leaned on the big guy's shoulders, and his tablemate silently scooted his chair back and left.

"You know," Kyle said. "I don't understand why you're sitting at our table."

"Yeah," Rhonda added. "Shouldn't you be hovering over the football stadium with 'Goodyear' written on you?"

They all laughed at that, Xander included. He was still laughing when he turned back to the table, and came face-to-face with Buffy's expression, which said she definitely didn't get the joke.

"Kid's fat," he said. *What more does she need?*

He looked at Willow and saw an expression of dismay. She didn't get it either.

The next day, Buffy met Rupert Giles for their scheduled sparring session.

Giles wore body armor and heavy, padded boxing gloves. Buffy wore gloves, no armor. But then, she was the one doing the punching and kicking. She was the Slayer. Giles was a librarian and a Watcher, not a warrior. His responsibility was to train the Slayer, guide her, direct her. Watch her. Getting the stuffing knocked out of him by her wasn't in the job description, hence the chest protector.

And His Tweedness was one of those very British types, she reflected, in whom there was a lot of stuffing.

She threw a right, a left, spun and came out of the spin with another right, spun again into a kick, then leapt into the air, kicking out with both feet at once into his gloves. Hitting hard, not holding back. Breathing hard, too.

She advanced on him again. He waved his gloves.

"Right," Giles said. "That's enough training for one day."

"Well, that last roundhouse was kind of sloppy. Sure you don't want to do it again?" Buffy asked.

"No, that's fine." He was breathing hard too. She'd seen Giles in action and knew he was pretty tough, for an old guy. But still, he was over forty, so what could one expect? "You run along to class," he panted, "while I wait for the feeling to return to my arms."

Class. That was the hard part about being the Slayer. Or, one of many. She had to be the Slayer; it wasn't like she'd auditioned for it, like cheerleader tryouts or anything. It demanded a lot from a girl. She could never just be one of the gang, never just hang out. The responsibility weighed heavily on her.

If the other kids in school were out all night, it was because they were having fun, or getting into mischief of some kind. In her case, it was just another night on the job, keeping the world safe from the bloodsucking undead. *And then I still have to go to class the next day.*

As Buffy neared a corner of the hallway, she heard a commotion from the other side. Students shrieked. And over it all, sounding somewhat strained, the unmistakable voice of Principal Flutie.

"Look out!" he cried. "It's gotten loose!"

There were more shrieks. They didn't sound terrified—and it was broad daylight—so her Slayer hackles didn't rise, but she was curious. She hurried toward the corner.

"Stop the beast!" Mr. Flutie called.

Then she rounded the corner and saw it, darting straight for her. A tiny pink piglet, running like pork chops were on the school lunch menu. Probably it was trying to get away from the ridiculous outfit someone had dressed it in. *Vandals, maybe.*

Buffy bent over and snagged the piglet, lifting it into her arms. The poor thing was wearing a tiny Sunnydale

High football helmet with papier-mâché tusks attached at the sides of his snout and had a row of green foam triangles stuck to its back, like a cartoon dinosaur's fins.

Mr. Flutie caught up to them. "Naughty Herbert," he said. "Gave Mr. Flutie quite a scare, didn't he?"

He drew himself up, addressing the students crowding the hallway. "Students, I'd like you all to meet Herbert, our new mascot for the Sunnydale High Razorbacks!" This was met with a smattering of applause.

"He's so cute!" Buffy said.

"He's *not* cute," Mr. Flutie insisted. "No, he's a fierce Razorback." He pumped his fists into the air, and there was some halfhearted clapping.

Buffy studied the poor, overaccessorized pig. "He doesn't look mean, Mr. Flutie."

"He's mean, he's ready for action." Mr. Flutie indicated Herbert's add-ons. "See, here are the tusks, and . . . a scary . . . razorback." The green fins. Now she got it.

"You're right," Buffy agreed. Sometimes a principal had to be humored. "He is a fine mascot and will engender school spirit."

"Well, he'd better—costs a fortune to feed him." He bent down, spoke directly to Herbert. "Let's get you back in your cage." He reached for the pig, and Herbert let out a squeal. Mr. Flutie backed off, gestured for Buffy to carry the new mascot.

"This way," he said. Buffy led the way, the piglet oinking contentedly in her arms.

Willow and Xander sat on one of the stone benches scattered around the campus, his geometry textbook open on her lap. He had a notebook and a pencil and was jotting numbers and lines down, but not really catching on. They were a study in contrast—red-haired Willow wearing a bright orange sweater over a patterned skirt, and Xander, dark-haired and eyed, all in shades of black and gray.

"I'm not getting this," Xander said.

"It's simple, really," Willow explained. She didn't understand why his patience seemed to be so short—as in, nonexistent—today. But she was willing to be extra patient with him to make up for it. "See, the bisector of a vertex is the line that divides the angle at that vertex into two equal parts."

"It's like a big blur, all these numbers and angles," he said, not really even listening to her. *There's enough going on in my head without filling it up with lame mathematical theory,* Xander thought. *I know the math I need. How fast, how strong, how mean? Calculations that matter.*

"It's the same stuff from last week. You had it down then."

"Why do I need to learn this?" he demanded.

" 'Cause otherwise you'll flunk math."

"Explain the part where that's bad."

They'd had this conversation before. "You remember," she said. "You fail math, you flunk out of school, you end up being the guy at the pizza place that sweeps the floor and says, 'Hey, kids, where's the cool parties this weekend?' We've been through this."

As she spoke, Xander rubbed the bridge of his nose. "Do you have a headache?" she asked, concerned. She touched his temple, gently, and he shook her hand away.

"Yeah," he said. "And I think I know what's causing it." He snatched the book off her lap and tossed it into a nearby garbage can. Smiling at his direct hit, he went on. "That's better. It goes right to the source of the pain."

"Xander—"

But he cut her off. *Enough is enough,* he thought. *Even just a little bit of this, that's still enough. No more.* "Look, forget it, okay? I don't get it. I won't ever. I don't care." He stood suddenly, throwing his spiral notebook into Willow's lap, and stormed away.

Willow had been friends with Xander a long time, and, frankly, had the hots for him almost as long. She was willing to overlook a lot of less-than-polite behavior from him. *Even this will pass,* she thought. "We can finish this another time," she suggested, but he was gone, beyond even hearing her.

Mr. Flutie showed Buffy to a classroom in which a cage was set up for Herbert.

"See, the problem is," he said as they walked, "you kids today have no school spirit. Hold on, let me get his outfit off." He removed Herbert's helmet and foam razorback. "Today it's all gangs and drugs and those movies on Showtime with the nudity." Looking at Buffy, he quickly added, "I don't have cable. I only heard."

More passionately, he went on. "When I was your age, we cared about the school's reputation, the team's record, all that stuff." Then, as if he realized what he was saying, he amended himself. "Of course, when I was your age I was surrounded by old guys telling me how much better things were when they were my age." He gave up then, and went in to prepare the cage for Herbert's arrival.

Buffy gave a small laugh. "Yeah," she said, more to Herbert than to Mr. Flutie. *For a principal, he isn't always as clueless as he seems,* she thought.

She was still standing there holding the pig when Xander entered the hallway through the double doors to outside. He didn't say anything, just gave her the slightest glance and gave Herbert a prolonged stare as he passed by. Which Buffy thought was odd, though not necessarily any more so than the rest of his behavior had been lately.

No, what really creeped her was that Xander gave the pig the wiggins. Herbert squealed, terrified, and wriggled in her arms like he wanted to beat his own personal best at the hundred-yard dash. It was all she could do just to hang on to him. He kept squealing and writhing until Xander was long out of sight.

Why would he be so afraid of Xander? she wondered. He wasn't that way with the rest of the kids in the hall—had kind of liked being the center of attention, it seemed. So what was it now that was so different? Something about Xander?

Harmless old Xander Harris? A pig-wigger? Couldn't be . . .

A sudden storm had rolled over Sunnydale during the day, unleashing driving rain and booming thunder. Rain had its pluses and minuses, but one of the big minuses was that P.E. had to be held indoors, in the big old gym. And Coach Herrold, not huge on imagination to begin with, had a limited repertoire of activities that he could think up for indoor workouts, especially once basketball season was over.

Coach Herrold was a big man with silver hair and a military bearing. Buffy had heard rumors that he'd served as a drill sergeant for years, finally getting out and becoming a high school coach because it was the only other place where he could command blind obedience.

"All right, it's raining," he said, marching up and back

between the two assembled ranks of P.E. students, resplendent in Sunnydale burgundy and gold. He carried a red rubber ball under his arm; others had already been handed out. "All regular gym classes have been postponed. So you know what that means . . . dodgeball." He held his ball up in one big fist, as if to demonstrate to anyone who hadn't caught on yet what a dodgeball looked like. "Now, for those of you who may have forgotten, the rules are as follows: you dodge."

He tossed his ball to Buffy, stepped out of the center, and blew his everpresent whistle. The two sides backed away from each other, toward opposite walls, students already eyeing their intended targets.

Coach Herrold blew the whistle again and rubber flew.

"One down," someone said as the first kid was tagged by one of the red balls. More went down quickly, stepping aside to the bench. To survive in dodgeball, you had to be light on your feet, with the reflexes to avoid the flying balls, yet still fast enough to grab any that came your way so you could knock out members of the opposing team. Buffy and Willow had both started with balls, but that only gave the most momentary of advantages.

Buffy had the distinct sense that she was being particularly targeted by Rhonda Kelley, but that was hard to know for sure in a game where everyone was, by definition, a target. Some people threw the ball harder than others, though, and Buffy dodged a couple of well-aimed burners that came uncomfortably close. Then she caught a glimpse of Xander winding up for a powerful throw. Before she even had a chance to wonder who he was targeting, she saw—Willow had just thrown a good one, followed through on her throw, and her back was mostly to Xander. His ball slammed into her shoulder, hard.

The look Willow tossed his way as she slunk toward the bench almost broke Buffy's heart. *What is up with him?* she wondered again.

But Buffy didn't have time to dwell on it. Her last teammate was knocked out, and she realized it was just she facing down six opponents.

And not just any six.

Xander, Kyle, Rhonda, Tor, Heidi, and Lance. Buffy flashed back on the Bronze, last night, and the zoo trip before that. *This is too weird,* she thought. She faced them for a moment, but then, almost as one, they turned away from her. Looked at Lance Lincoln. Held the look.

Lance returned it, very nervous.

Kyle threw the first ball. Hard, at close range. Lance went down on the wooden gym floor. Kyle scooped up another ball, slammed Lance again. Then they were all throwing balls, pounding Lance into the floor like they wanted to nail him to it.

Buffy ran, across no-man's land and into the middle of it all. She took Lance's hand, hoisted him to his feet and away from the punishing balls. A couple of balls bounced harmlessly now, but no one was throwing any more. They were just looking at Buffy silently. She caught Xander's gaze, stared into his eyes as if hoping to see something there. Some glimmer of the Xander she had known.

But there was nothing. He was a stranger. He turned away, and his new friends followed.

Game over. A satisfactory class session, at least to one person. "God, this game is brutal," Coach Herrold said as they filed out. "I love it."

* * *

Willow waited outside the gym for Xander. She leaned against a bank of lockers, and when he came out he was accompanied by Kyle, Tor, Heidi, and Rhonda. They were all dressed in dark, blacks and browns, almost like a uniform.

"Xander," she said, stepping toward him. "What's wrong with you?"

With a glance back toward his friends, he moved away from them. He took Willow's elbow and drew her to one side. "I guess you've noticed that I've been different around you, lately," he said, his voice low and intimate.

"Yes."

"I think, um . . ." he paused, as if searching for the right words. "I think it's because my feelings for you have been changing."

Her heart skipped a beat. *Depending on how he meant that . . .*

"Well, we've been friends for such a long time," he went on, "that I feel like I need to tell you something." Willow's heart soared. *Is this going to be what I've always wanted to hear from Xander? I want you to go out with me on Friday night, he might say. I want you to marry me. Do you like big families?* She waited, expectant, hope swelling in her.

Xander continued, his tone serious. "I've . . . I've decided to drop geometry. So . . . I won't be needing your math help anymore."

Willow could feel her hope collapsing, her face falling. She struggled to hold it together. "Which means," Xander said, raising his voice so his friends could hear, "I won't have to look at your pasty face again."

He started to laugh then, and the others joined in. The group of them sounded sick to her, laughing so hard at such a mean joke. Willow's heart sank. Her eyes filling with tears, she turned and walked away, barely registering the sight of her best friend Buffy standing at her locker. As she hurried down the corridor the sound of their laughter rang in her ears, like church bells summoning mourners for a funeral.

Buffy slammed her locker. *I'm willing to excuse Xander a lot,* she thought, *for Will's sake. But this is too much.* She stormed up to him, looked him in the eye.

"You gonna say something to me?" she asked.

He just started laughing again, the high-pitched, manic laugh that he and his newfound chums seemed to share. They all cracked up, and Xander joined them. They disappeared down the hall, only their wicked laughter lingering behind them.

It was a new sensation, strolling the campus like you owned it. Like you were the big dogs, and all the puppies got out of your way. Xander liked the way it felt. He felt powerful. He couldn't remember ever having been quite so alive. Senses sharp, muscles honed, mind alert. And his friends had his back; Kyle and Rhonda, Tor, Heidi. He'd started thinking of them as a pack, animals on the hunt.

I'm not sure what we're hunting, he thought. *But I'll know it when I find it.* He was confident of that.

He stopped, and they stopped with him. As one. Each responsive to the others' slightest signals.

Xander sniffed the air. Picked up a scent.

"Dogs," he said.

"Where?" Kyle asked. Xander nodded his head, and then led the way again, toward the campus picnic tables.

At one table, three guys were eating hot dogs and

talking music. Xander knew one of them, Adam somebody. He wasn't important enough to have a last name. He wasn't one of the pack.

"You're out of your mind," Adam was saying as they approached. "That's no way to play lead guitar. That's just hunt 'n' peck."

Xander stopped next to the table, and his friends fanned out around it. Adam saw them. "Hey, Xander," he said. "You've seen Wretched Refuse. What do you think of the guy who plays lead?"

The question was too inane to deserve an answer. Xander ignored him, and watched as Heidi and Tor leaned over the table, snatching hot dogs—no bun, just the meat—from two of the guys' plates.

"Hey," Adam protested. "Hey, what are you guys—"

Rhonda cut him off. "Shut up."

"You're *sharing,*" Kyle said, voice like ice.

"Friends *like* to share," Xander added.

Heidi and Tor took big bites of their "shared" dogs.

"Good?" Xander asked.

"It's too well done," Tor said, tossing his dog back onto Adam's tray. Heidi threw hers down as well.

"Hey," Adam said. He sounded offended, as if there was some reason for his existence other than to provide for Xander and his friends. "That is not cool."

But Xander had already caught another scent on the air. His head snapped around, and he started away from Adam and his lunch companions like they weren't even there. The others followed, Kyle stepping up and over the picnic table and scattering lunch trays as he went.

Xander led them into the school building, following his nose. The scent grew stronger as they stalked the halls, headed directly toward their prey. Something weak, something that could be brought down by the pack.

Or rather, the Pack, Xander thought, suddenly realizing that it should be capitalized.

The scent drew them to a classroom. Xander opened the door, and they walked in. There was no one inside, just a cage. And in the cage, a small pink piglet. Succulent, juicy, tempting. Xander knelt beside the cage, looked at the little pig.

"Let's do lunch," he said.

CHAPTER 3

He could feel everything, every sensation. The sun on his cheek. The slightest breeze flicking his hair. The sidewalk beneath the balls of his feet. He could smell perfume on a girl all the way across the quad. He could hear whispered conversations a block away.

But there was no reason to. None of those people meant anything to him. None of them mattered. Only the Pack mattered.

They roamed the campus like it was their birthright. Xander reveled in the sidelong glances, the looks of outright fear from those they passed. He was an object of terror, he thought, and it tasted sweet. At one point, they converged on Lance, who cringed and ducked out of their way. They let him go . . . he was beneath real notice.

Finally, something interesting caught his attention. They sat on a low wall on the second floor. Their backs were to him, but that didn't matter. If he hadn't recognized them, he still would have known their voices, their smells. Buffy and Willow. He listened.

"I've known him my whole life, Buffy. We haven't always been close, but . . . he's never . . ." Willow's voice caught. She turned to face Buffy, tears rimming her eyes.

"I think something's wrong with him," Buffy said.

"Or maybe there's something wrong with me," Willow countered.

"What are you talking about?"

"Come on," Willow said. "He's not picking on you. He's just sniffing you a lot. I don't know, so maybe three isn't company anymore."

"You think this has something to do with me?" Buffy asked. Knowing there was only one thing that could mean. She'd known Xander had had a crush on her practically since her first day in Sunnydale. But that didn't make sense—he'd have to know that being mean to Willow wouldn't get him anywhere with her.

"Of course."

Buffy shook her head. "No," she said firmly. "That still doesn't explain why he's hanging out with the dode patrol." She slid down from the wall. "Something's going on. Something weird." She started past Willow.

Her friend turned to watch her go. "What are you going to do?"

Buffy turned to face Willow once more. "Gonna talk to the expert on weird."

That expert could only be Giles, who she found in his usual haunt, the school library.

He'd been cataloguing, she figured, because he was carrying a clipboard and one of those little cards from the card catalogue with him as he moved from place to place.

While he was cataloguing—she didn't know if that was the right verb, but guessed it would do—she was talking and following him around. And finding him somewhat less than sympathetic.

"Xander's taken to teasing the less fortunate?"

"Uh-huh," Buffy said.

"There's been a noticeable change in both clothing and demeanor?"

"Yes."

"And spends all his spare time lounging about with imbeciles?" Giles opened a card catalogue drawer, looked into it as if he'd lost something there.

"It's bad, isn't it?"

"It's devastating," Giles agreed. "He's turned into a sixteen-year-old boy." Giles shut the drawer again. "Of course, you'll have to kill him."

"Giles, I'm serious," Buffy said.

Giles crossed the room to another cabinet. "So am I, except for the part about killing him." He looked at Buffy and stopped, as if realizing that he owed her a more detailed explanation. "Testosterone is the great equalizer; it turns all men into morons," he said. "He will, however, get over it."

"I can't believe that you, of all people, are trying to Scully me," Buffy argued. "There's something supernatural at work." She grabbed some books from on top of the cabinet, shoved them toward Giles. "Get your books! Look stuff up!"

Giles took the books from her hand, replaced them in their proper spot. "Look under what?"

"I don't know," Buffy moaned. "That's your department."

"The evidence you've presented me with is sketchy at best," Giles said. Buffy could feel the argument being lost.

"He scared the pig!" she insisted, with a sudden flailing gesture.

Giles gave her a get-real look.

"Well, he did."

"Buffy, boys can be cruel." Lecturing, now. "They tease, they prey on the weak. It's a natural teen behavior pattern."

"What did you just say?"

"Uh, what?" Giles stammered. "Um, they tease—"

Buffy interrupted him. "They prey on the weak. I heard that somewhere." Then she remembered where. *That zookeeper.* "Xander has been acting totally wiggy since we went to the zoo. Him and Kyle and all those guys went into the hyena cage . . . Oh God, that laugh—"

"Are you saying Xander's becoming a hyena?" Giles asked. He didn't seem to give her theory much credence, considering some of the things they had been through together.

"I don't know," Buffy said. "Or been possessed by one. Not just Xander, all of them."

Giles shook his head, tugging on his ear. *He still isn't buying it,* Buffy knew. "Well, I've certainly never heard of—"

Then Willow charged into the library, clearly upset. *Now what's Xander done?* Buffy found herself wondering.

"Herbert," Willow exclaimed. "They found him!"

"The pig?" Buffy asked.

"Dead," Willow replied. "And also, eaten! Principal Flutie's freaking out."

Buffy looked at Giles. "Testosterone, huh?"

He avoided her glance and headed for the stacks.

"What are you gonna do?" Willow asked him.

"Get my books," he answered. "Look stuff up."

Mr. Flutie found them lounging on a picnic table. DuFours, Kelley, Hauer, and Barrie. He knew each of them well, on a personal basis. He was very familiar with their permanent records. These were the kind of kids every principal had nightmares about, the ones who only came to school because they had to and lived to make trouble for the administration. They weren't stupid, but they were aggressively unteachable. You couldn't motivate them because they only understood power and money, and a high school principal didn't have enough of either.

"You four!" he shouted.

Kyle DuFours looked up lazily. "What?"

He was too angry to beat around the bush. "Oh, don't think I don't know," he said. "Three kids saw you outside Herbert's room. You're busted. Yeah. You're going down."

"How is Herbert?" Rhonda Kelley asked.

"Crunchy," Heidi Barrie responded. The others broke into cackling laughter.

No respect at all. He couldn't take any more. "That's it. My office, right now."

They just sat there, looking at him. The laughter had faded, but he could feel the chilliness of their stares. "Now!" he demanded.

Kyle got up first, and the others followed his lead. Mr. Flutie marched them ahead of himself, toward the building. "You're gonna have so much detention," he threatened, "your grandchildren'll be staying after school."

* * *

Hanging out in the library has had one positive effect on Buffy, Willow thought. It had taught her how to do research, when it needed to be done. *Like now.* Willow loved research, but getting Buffy together with a book was sometimes a challenge, and other times was not even in the realm of possibility.

Buffy sat on the steps leading up to the stacks, a huge folio across her lap. Willow sat at a table, reading one of her own. She looked up when Buffy spoke. "Wow," Buffy said. "Apparently Noah rejected hyenas from the Ark because he thought they were an evil, impure mixture of dogs and cats."

"Hyenas aren't well-liked," Willow agreed.

"They do seem to be the shmoes of the animal kingdom," Buffy said, bringing the book down to show Willow a picture.

"Why couldn't Xander be possessed by a puppy?" Willow asked. "Or some ducks?"

"That's assuming 'possession' is the right word," Buffy said.

"Oh, I'd say it is," Giles offered. He emerged from another part of the library, yet another book in his hands. "The Masai of the Serengeti have spoken of animal possession for generations. I should have remembered that."

"So how does it work?" Buffy asked.

"Well," he explained, "apparently there's a sect of animal worshippers, known as Primals. They believe that humanity—consciousness, the soul—is a perversion, a dilution of spirit. To them, the animal state is holy. They're able, through transpossession, to draw the spirit of certain animals into themselves."

"And then they start acting like hyenas."

"Only the most predatory animals were of interest to Primals," Giles said. "So yes, that would fit."

"So what happens to the person once the spirit is in them?" Buffy asked.

"If it goes unchecked?" Giles said. Instead of answering, he handed Buffy the massive volume he carried.

She looked at the page he showed her, horror creeping over her face as she did. She slammed the book shut, put it down on the table next to Willow, and headed for the door. "I gotta find Xander," she said.

Willow reached for the book, tugged it to herself, flipped it open to the page Giles had shown Buffy. An old engraving on the page seemed to show a feast of some kind. But the main course didn't look to Willow like hyena chow, or even raw piglet. It was humans—missing arms, legs, even heads, all depicted in graphic and gory detail. *Ewww,* she thought. *I hope Cavalry Buffy's not too late to save the day.*

Buffy found the classroom to which she'd delivered Herbert before. The door was open. Inside, the cage Mr. Flutie had bought for Herbert was bent and twisted apart; the heavy wire looked as if animals had been at it. *In a way . . .*

They are strong, she said to herself, moving around the wreckage. The floor, she realized, was littered with straw from the cage—and something else. She bent over, picked one up. It was almost eight inches long, a little bigger around than her finger. Broken at the end, as if something had snapped it—or bit it, maybe in search of marrow.

"Pig bones," she said.

She put it back in the mess on the floor and stood to leave. There was nothing more to learn here. She turned . . .

And there he was, right behind her. His face held a malicious grin.

"Xander."

He didn't speak, just took a step closer to her. She sidestepped, to go around him, but he moved to block her. Obviously he wasn't going to just let her pass, so she tried another approach.

"This is ridiculous," she said. "We need to talk—" Only instead of talking, she leapt at him, hands at his shoulders, driving him backward. He went down, and she landed on his chest, driving him into the floor.

He just laughed. "I've been waiting for you to jump my bones," he said.

The four perps stood in Mr. Flutie's office, and he paced before them, in front of his desk. "I have seen some sick things in my life, believe me, but this is beyond the pale," he sputtered. He was still enraged by the vicious attack on Herbert. "What is it with you people? Is it drugs? How could you—a poor defenseless pig . . ."

Then he realized, with some trepidation, that they were getting closer, and he certainly wasn't moving toward them. Students should be kept at arm's length, he believed. *And long arms, at that.* But these four were approaching him—encircling him. And they had started to make strange, almost subvocal noises—meaningless, animal sounds.

He fought to keep his nerves under control, his voice from betraying his fear. "What are you doing?" he demanded as they surrounded him.

Xander growled an animalistic snarl and heaved, catching Buffy by surprise with a strength she didn't know he had. He bucked her off of him and spun her over, so that she was on her back, looking up into his face. He pinned her wrists to the tiled floor.

"Get off of me!"

"Is that what you really want?" he asked. She tried to hurl him off, but he was strong—even for her, the Slayer. *Pretty much confirms Giles's theory,* she thought. She gave an extra push, testing herself, really, to see if she was holding back because he was Xander, a friend. *A hyena-possessed friend, maybe, but a friend just the same.* "We both know what you really want," he went on. "You want danger, don't you? You like your men dangerous."

"You're in trouble, Xander," Buffy tried. "You are infected with some hyena thing. It's like a demonic possession—"

Xander ignored her, cutting her off as if she hadn't even spoken. "Dangerous and mean, right? Like Angel, your mystery guy. Well, guess who just got mean?"

When they actually touched him, Mr. Flutie lost his cool. "Now, stop that!" he shouted. "You're only gonna make things worse for yourselves."

He moved away from them, behind his desk. Rhonda followed him back there, but at least kept her distance. Kyle and Heidi filled in the space on the other side, so he was trapped behind the desk. Panic was building in him, but he was still in charge of the situation, he knew. He was still the authority figure. He held the trump card, and it was time to play it.

"Okay, I'll tell you how this is going to work," he said, straightening out his dark sports coat, trying to look casual. "I'm going to call your parents and they are going to take you all home."

He reached for the phone, but Tor was there first, pressing the receiver down against the cradle. After a moment, though, he handed the receiver to Mr. Flutie.

"Thank you," Mr. Flutie said.

Trump card. When all else fails, call the—

Rhonda swatted the telephone from his hand and the unit crashed against the wall.

"Sorry," Rhonda said.

"That is *it!*" Mr. Flutie yelled. He spun away from Rhonda to go around the desk and leave the office. Authority was one thing, but these kids were beyond anything he could do. He'd been uncomfortable from the start, but that had escalated quickly into fear and was now just a hair's breadth from abject terror. A quick call to the Sunnydale P.D., though, and they'd be someone else's problem.

But Kyle and Heidi were still on that side of the desk. As he neared Kyle, the boy leaned forward and unleashed a hideous roar, sounding more like a wild beast than a high school student. Mr. Flutie, startled, fell back into his swiveling desk chair.

"Do you know how long I've waited?" Xander asked. "Until you'd stop pretending that we aren't attracted—" As he spoke, he released one wrist, caressed her blond hair gently with his hand. The way a lover would.

Buffy took full advantage of his distraction. With the help of her free hand, she was able to throw him off her and scramble to her feet. He stood, and came toward her again, barely even breaking stride in his sentence.

"Until Willow stops kidding herself that I could settle with anyone but you—"

"I don't wanna hurt you, Xander," Buffy said, backing away from his relentless advance.

But it was bluff, and she knew it. She couldn't bring herself to really hurt Xander. She just hoped he wouldn't realize that.

He didn't. He lunged, slamming her backward into a vending machine. Someone's long-lost change clinked down into the coin return.

"Now do you wanna hurt me?" Xander asked. "C'mon, Slayer—I like it when you're scared." She struggled against him but he held her tight, sniffing the air around her. "The more I scare you, the better you smell."

Then Xander stopped talking, forced his head in between Buffy's jaw and shoulders, and began to savagely kiss her neck.

Rhonda and Heidi were touching him, fingers running across his arms, his neck, his shoulders. Touching between principals and students was a major bad thing, in Mr. Flutie's personal rule book. *I'm not sure this exact situation is covered in the Education Department's guidelines,* he thought. *But in concept . . .*

"You're about *this* close to expulsion, people." He rose, trying once more to force his way through the four grunting problem cases. "But I'm willing to talk to the school counselor, and we can discuss options—"

Heidi shoved him back into his chair. And then Tor leapt up to the surface of his desk and squatted there, snarling, looking for all the world like a jungle creature ready to spring.

"Get down from there this instant!" Mr. Flutie commanded, putting every reserve he had into not falling to the ground and begging for mercy. He'd taught school and had been a principal, for years, but he'd never been so scared.

Rhonda closed in on the other side of him, fingers splayed far apart. She raked her nails across his cheek. He felt them cutting into his flesh.

"Oh!" he called out. He touched the torn skin and drew his hand away, seeing his own blood on his palm. "Are you insane?"

The students' grunts and groans intensified as they closed in, as if drawn by the scent of freshly spilled blood, or the sight of Mr. Flutie finally giving in to his terror. These weren't just troubled youth, they were something more than that. *Something much, much worse,* he thought.

And then Tor attacked, springing from the desk like a cat, snarling and vicious. He drove Mr. Flutie back into his chair, and before he knew it, the others were on him as well, and they were laughing hysterically, laughing and clawing and tearing, and the last thing he knew before he lost consciousness was that he had been wrong. He had always contended that there were no bad kids, only troubled ones. But that's what these kids were, just plain bad, and there would be no reasoning with them, no detention or expulsion that would straighten them out. It didn't really matter to him anymore because, if they were ever going to become productive members of society, he wouldn't be around to see it.

Chapter 4

School had long since let out, and darkness had descended on Sunnydale. Willow sat alone in the shadowed library, at one of the computer workstations Giles had reluctantly agreed to allow in his sanctuary. On the screen before her was video footage of a pack of hyenas. They were terrifying to watch as they savagely tore at their prey, a wildebeest they had brought down. She had always thought of hyenas as scavengers, but it turned out they were fierce predators, hunting in packs and going after the weak, the infirm—easy targets, in other words.

Not brave animals, necessarily. But deadly ones. And not the cute jokesters they had been made out to be in the cartoons.

The door opened and Buffy entered, dragging a heavy load behind her. "Hurry up!" she called to Willow. "We've gotta lock him up somehow, before he comes to."

Not just any heavy load, Willow realized. "Omigod, Xander—what happened?"

"I hit him," Buffy answered.

There was a locking book cage in the library, for rarer books and manuscripts and some of Giles's occult tomes that he didn't want to fall into the hands of the wrong people—like, anyone but himself and maybe the Slayerettes. Buffy headed for the cage, Willow alongside, looking for signs of damage on Xander. Only the tiniest part of her was vengeful enough to hope there was at least a good-sized bruise or bump. He was out cold, but she couldn't see any signs of impact.

"With what?" she asked, opening the cage door.

"A desk," Buffy replied, hauling him into the cage. "He tried his hand at felony sexual assault."

"Oh, Buffy," Willow said, horrified. "The hyena in him didn't—"

"No. No, but it's safe to say that in his animal state, his idea of wooing somebody doesn't include a Yanni CD and a bottle of Chianti." Buffy came out of the cage, closed the door behind her, turned the key. She jingled the keys in her hand as she crossed to a desk. "There, that oughta hold him. Where's Giles?"

"He got a call to some teacher's meeting," Willow told her. Buffy took a big swallow from a bottle of water. *Beating up your friends must be thirsty work,* Willow guessed. "What are we going to do?" she asked. "I mean, how do we get Xander back?"

That didn't seem high on Buffy's list of concerns. "Right now," she said, "I'm worried about what the rest of the pack are up to."

Giles walked in just then. "The rest of the pack were spotted outside Herbert the mascot's cage. They were sent to the principal's office."

"Good. That'll show 'em," Willow said. The look on Giles's face wasn't reassuring. "Did it show 'em?"

"They didn't hurt him, did they?" Buffy asked.

"They, uh, ate him."

Willow sank into a chair.

"They ate Principal Flutie?" Buffy said.

"Ate him up?" Willow added.

"The official theory is that wild dogs got into his office somehow," Giles said. "There was no one at the scene."

Willow found the bright spot—*A tiny one, but bright just the same,* she thought. Hoped. "But Xander didn't—he was with you," she said to Buffy.

"Oh," Giles said, seeing the unconscious boy in the cage for the first time. "Well, that's a small mercy."

"Giles, how do we stop this?" Buffy asked. "How do you transpossess someone?" Buffy, as usual, was looking for solutions while everyone else was still focused on the problem. It was one of the things Willow loved about her friend, the Slayer.

"I'm afraid I still don't have all the pieces," Giles replied. "Accounts of the Primals and their methods are a bit thin on the ground. There is some talk of a predatory act, but the exact ritual is . . ." He shook his head, and picked up one of his massive books. He flipped to a certain page, and continued. "The 'Malleus Maleficarum' deals with the particulars of demonic possession, which may apply."

He put the book down on the table, flipping a few more pages. "Yes, one should be able to transfer the spirits to another human—"

"Oh, thanks, great," Buffy interrupted. "Any volunteers?"

"Oh," he said, his voice small. "Good point."

Buffy went on. "What we need to do is put the hyena back in the hyena."

"But, until we know more—" Giles began.

Buffy was onto something, an idea, and Willow got a little thrill from watching her dog its trail. "Betcha that zookeeper can help us. Maybe he didn't quarantine those hyenas 'cause they were sick."

Giles seemed to catch on. "We should talk to him."

Propelled by her own enthusiasm, Buffy started for the door, then stopped again. "Oh, wait," she said. "Somebody's gotta watch Xander."

Willow stood. "I will."

"Are you sure?" Buffy asked. "If he wakes up—"

"I'll be all right. Go." Willow's voice was firm. She held her hand out, and Buffy put the cage keys in it.

"Come on," she said to Giles. They left, and Willow was alone again, in the dark library.

Except for Xander, still out cold in the cage. She tucked the keys into the pocket of her skirt.

Jessamyn walked through the park almost every night. The Southern California climate let her do that, not like where she'd moved from, in Michigan, where the winters were long and kept her inside most of the time. Here, the evening was cool but refreshing, and she liked the walk, the feel of the grass under her tennies, the bounce of the baby in his backpack, moving and breathing and sometimes gurgling against her back. These walks had helped her keep her sanity, stay centered after having him, and she thought he liked them too.

But tonight's was different.

There were buildings, not a hundred feet away. People in them, having dinner, watching TV, reading, bathing their kids.

Here, beneath shadows cast by moonlight on the bushes, four young people slept on the grass, huddled against each other. They looked like puppies in a box.

Only, not so cute.

She'd give them a wide berth. *They look like high school kids,* Jessamyn thought. *But, strange ones.*

Suddenly, eyes flashed silver in the moonlight.

They were awake.

Moving, their muscles fluid, like liquid beneath their skin.

And even worse, growling, low throaty sounds under their breath.

Looking at her.

And, she realized, *looking at the baby.*

Two boys, two girls. She wasn't sure which looked meaner.

Forget the wide berth. She backed away, back toward the buildings, toward the direction from which she'd come, until she felt she'd put some distance between them, and then she turned and ran.

Afraid they were coming after her, padding silently like wolves, she risked a glance over her shoulder.

But they weren't there. They were settling in, as if their nap had been interrupted but they were going back to it. Already losing interest in her.

She had liked these walks, through the park.

She knew she never would again.

"Willow."

It was Xander's voice, from the cage. Willow paused the hyena video. *Which,* she admitted to herself, *is morbidly fascinating. If yucky.*

She turned to face him. "How are you feeling?"

He tossed her a wry grin. "Like somebody hit me with

a desk." He looked around the cage, registering where he was for the first time. "What am I doing here?"

Awkward question. "You're . . . resting." *Awkward answer, too.* She walked toward the cage.

Xander rose, hooking the cage screen with his fingers. "You guys got me locked up now?"

" 'Cause you're sick. Buffy said—"

"Oh, yeah," Xander said, disgusted. "Buffy had her all-purpose solution: punch 'em out and knock 'em down. I'd love to see what she'd do to somebody who was really sick."

"That's not fair," Willow argued. "Buffy's saved both our lives."

"Before she showed up, our lives didn't need that much saving, did they?" Xander said. He had a point, she had to admit. She couldn't remember a time her life had been in immediate peril of being snuffed out, before Buffy. Since then, there had been several occasions. "Weren't things a lot simpler when it was just you and me?"

"Maybe . . ." But then again, there had always been strange deaths and unexplained disappearances in Sunnydale. The town was on a hellmouth, after all. Buffy showing up hadn't made it worse. Willow and Xander had just become involved a little more personally—*But by choice,* she reminded herself. *We volunteered for Scooby duty. It's not like she drafted us.*

"When we were alone together," he went on. She liked the sound of that—hoped she didn't like it too much. "Willow," he sighed, "I know there's something wrong with me. I think it's getting worse. I can't just stand around waiting for Buffy to decide it's time to punch me out again. I want you to help me. I want you."

She *really* liked the sound of that. "I am helping you."

"You're doing what you're told."

"Buffy's trying to help you too, you know that," Willow countered. "Or, Xander does."

"Yeah, Buffy's so selfless, always thinking of us. Well, if I'm so dangerous, how come she left you alone with me?" Xander's voice was low and warm—almost as if the cage between them was fading away, and they were the only two people in the world.

Which was pretty close to what she'd always wanted.

Too close . . .

"I told her to."

"Why?" Xander asked.

"Because I know you better than she does," Willow answered. "And I wanted to be here to see if you were still you."

"You know I am. Look at me." She did, and she saw Xander. The boy she'd known most of her life. The boy she had always harbored dreams of being with. Of dating, marrying, growing old with. "Look," he said again.

She moved closer to the cage, wanting to touch him, smooth his hair, kiss his cheek where it was red from being hit.

Which was when he lunged, shoving his arm through an opening in the cage's doorway. Reaching for the keys dangling from her skirt pocket.

She jerked back, avoiding his grasp.

"Now I know," she said, with resignation.

Xander lost all pretense of intimacy, of friendship. He pounded at the cage with his fists. "Let me out!" he screamed, fury in his voice. "Let me out!"

The zookeeper's office was bigger than Buffy expected. He seemed to know his stuff. There were diplomas and certificates of honor on the wall, as well as photographs, African masks and weapons, and other memorabilia. In the center of the room he had a light table. Transparencies were laid on top of it, and the light from below shone up through them, making them easier to see.

For Giles, anyway, who seemed to know what he was looking at. They were meaningless to her.

". . . the students have been possessed by the hyenas," the zookeeper was saying. His manner was somehow reassuring, his voice level and calm.

"Yes," Giles said.

"Are you sure?"

"We're really, really sure," Buffy replied.

"You don't seem enormously surprised by this," Giles suggested.

"The zoo imported those hyenas from Africa," the zookeeper said. "There was something strange about them from day one. I did some homework. That particular breed is very rare. Totally vicious. Historically, they were worshipped by these guys—"

"The Primals," Giles offered.

"Yeah. Creepy guys. Now they had rituals for taking the hyenas' spirits, but I don't see how that could have happened to your kids."

"We don't know exactly how the ritual works," Giles said. "We know it involves a predatory act and some kind of symbol."

"A predatory act. Of course. That makes sense. Where did you read that?"

Giles seemed to sense a kindred spirit. "Do you have Sherman Jeffries's work on cults and—"

Giles can go on for days with this stuff, Buffy thought. *Better get back on track.* "Boys!" she interrupted.

"Sorry," Giles said.

The zookeeper glanced at his watch. "Look, I think we may have enough information so that together we can pull off a reverse transpossession."

"What do we do?" Buffy asked.

"You gotta get those possessed students to the hyena cage right away," he said. "I'll meet you there and we can begin the ritual."

"Well, we can guarantee you one of them," Buffy said. "But there're four more and we don't know where they are."

"I wouldn't worry about that," the zookeeper explained. "After hyenas feed and rest, they will track the missing member of their pack until they find him. They should come right to you."

Buffy caught Giles's glance. "Willow," she breathed.

Xander paced in the cage like—*Okay, why deny it? Like a caged animal.* Willow was keeping her distance, now. He'd made his move, and she had dodged him, and now the keys to this trap were across the room.

To make it worse, she was watching hyena video, over and over again. He could see the screen, hear the laughter of the pack on tape. He could almost smell the blood, taste the raw flesh. But just almost.

"Willow . . ." he said.

She glanced over her shoulder at him. "I'm not listening." Turned back to the screen. She didn't even want to look at him. *Well, that's okay with me. I don't want to look at her either. Just want that key.*

Another boy wouldn't have heard the faintest scuffling sounds from outside the library, wouldn't have caught the scent on the other side of the windows. But Xander wasn't another boy. He was something else, now.

Something more. He'd been transformed. He heard, he smelled. And the scent was familiar.

When he heard the voice, that was familiar too. Soft, taunting.

"Wil-lowww . . ." it said.

The Pack.

CHAPTER 5

They had come for him.

"Wil-lowww . . ." The voice belonged to Kyle. Xander had known they wouldn't just let him rot in here. They were his friends. *His real friends. Not the losers he'd grown up with, or Buffy, the so-called Slayer.* The Pack were the ones who really cared about what happened to him.

"Xander, shut up," Willow said.

"Wil-lowww . . ." Kyle called again.

Xander saw her shoulders tense as she realized the voice wasn't his. She didn't have time to react more than that, because suddenly they were crashing through the library windows. Glass rained onto the floor.

She leapt from her seat and ran out the door, like the coward he'd long suspected she was.

He kicked at the cage. Anxious to be free, on the prowl again.

They came for him. The Pack. They tugged at the cage, their combined strength breaking the heavy wire screen, tearing and bending until they ripped the door from its very hinges.

Xander was free.

The Pack came to him, surrounded him. They sniffed each other, touched each other the way members of a Pack do.

Yes, he was home, with them.

But, he realized, she was out there somewhere. Willow. Loose on the school grounds. She was scared, but she could still be dangerous to them. To the Pack. She had to be found, and stopped.

Xander led the hunt.

Willow turned a corner, ran to the first classroom door she saw. Grabbed the knob.

Locked.

Oh, no, she thought. She could hear the sounds from the library, knew the cage had been breached. Knew they were on their way.

And they ate Principal Flutie. And even Herbert.

Xander's with them now, but Xander isn't really Xander.

If they catch me . . .

She crossed the hall to another door. This one opened. She darted inside, shutting the door quietly behind her. *Who knows how well they can hear?*

Or smell?

Inside the darkened room, she threaded her way between the desks, crawled into the footwell of the teacher's desk, and pulled the chair into position in front of her.

It wasn't much, but it looked like the best she could do.

At the intersection, the Pack split up. Kyle, Rhonda, and Tor each went in different directions. Heidi followed Xander.

He smelled the air.

If there was one thing he knew, after all these years, it was Willow's scent.

That door.

Heidi sniffed, maybe catching it too.

Xander opened the door.

The room was dark. Quiet. He and Heidi walked among the desks, alert. Sniffing.

Willow remained crouched under the desk. She knew someone was in the room. No telling who. She heard soft footfalls. Someone breathing.

Then footsteps receding, and the door closing.

Safe.

She'd done it. Now she just had to find help.

She shoved the chair back, came out of her hiding place.

Xander was waiting. Heidi had moved on, but he'd stayed here, convinced she was in the room. *If there was one thing he knew . . .*

She started when she saw him, gasped. He gave a little roar and lunged at her, across the teacher's desk.

She evaded him, and ran.

He gave chase, but she upended a chair as she went, and he tripped over it.

Hit the floor.

She reached the door, flung it open.

Into Heidi's arms.

Willow screamed. Heidi growled, forcing the girl back into the room. Where Xander waited.

This had been a long time coming.

Heidi made a fine target. Totally focused on Willow, she didn't even see Buffy swing the fire extinguisher at her head. The metal made a satisfying clang against her skull, and she crumpled.

Giles tugged Willow to safety, out in the hall.

Relative safety, anyway.

There was still Xander.

He charged the doorway. Buffy brought the fire extinguisher up again. But it was a feint. He dodged the extinguisher, and she kicked out, catching him in the chest, knocking him backward.

Twice in one day she'd had to indulge in some Xander-bashing. *Not without its charms . . .*

But there was a noise in the hallway, at the intersection. The other three members of Xander's pack, converging there. They saw Buffy, Willow, and Giles. Charged.

"Run," Giles shouted.

They dashed into another classroom, and Buffy slammed the door shut. She held the knob.

On the other side, she could feel them yanking it, trying to turn it. They pounded on the heavy wooden door, growling angrily.

After a few moments of that, the barrage stopped and she heard their footsteps moving away.

"I think they're going," she said.

"They could be faking it," Willow suggested. Buffy understood her friend's fear—she felt terrible for having left Willow alone in such a vulnerable position. She couldn't be everywhere—but that didn't prevent her from feeling like she should be.

She tried to reassure Willow. "No, they're hungry. They'll be looking for somebody weak." *Which is not us.* "I'm really really sorry, Willow," she continued. "I didn't know they'd come after Xander."

"It's okay," Willow said.

Giles caught his breath. "We must lead them back to the zoo if we're going to stop this."

"Yeah, and before their next meal," Buffy said. "That's my job."

"Individually, they're almost as strong as you," Giles protested. "As a group—"

"They're tough," Buffy said. "But I think they're getting stupider. You guys go to the zoo and I'll bring them to you." She opened the door and went out into the night.

Hope I'm right, she thought.

Visiting friends was supposed to be fun, Rich Anderson believed. But they were barely out the door before Melissa started in on him.

"I didn't say she looked better than you," he insisted. "I said she looked better." *Okay, lame.* But he had to make an effort.

"I heard what I heard," Melissa said. She stopped on the walk, looked down at her son shoving a Twinkie into his mouth. "Joey, chew," she said. "You have to chew or you'll choke."

Little Joey nodded.

They all got into the sport-utility vehicle, pulling their doors shut behind themselves. He couldn't wait to get home. Maybe by then she'd have moved on.

"I don't see why we have to have this conversation every time we see them," he said.

"I didn't start it," Melissa answered. Her voice dripped icicles. Maybe she wouldn't move on so quickly after all.

Rich patted his pockets. "Damn," he said. "Where are the keys?"

"Huh?" she asked.

And then, as they sat there in the suddenly quiet car, they heard it—a soft, feminine voice, calling.

"Jo-eeey . . . Jo-eeey . . ."

The Andersons looked at each other, the fight forgotten. *What was that? Who was that?*

Suddenly a head appeared outside Joey's window—looking down, from on top of the car. The head roared, and then there were more of them. They were all over the car, banging on it with fists, growling at them through the windows. Rich clicked the locks shut—just in time, since they were grabbing at the door handles.

There were four of them, he thought, but there could have been more. It was dark, and they were moving, banging on the car here and then just as suddenly pressing their faces against the glass there. Shaking the big SUV, and roaring like wild beasts. Melissa was screaming, and in the back, Joey seemed petrified.

"Hey!" Rich shouted. "What's going on?"

Surely someone will call the cops, he thought. *All we have to do is wait here with the doors locked, until—*

One of them smashed through the back passenger window. Next to Joey. Arms reached in, grabbed for the boy. He held on to his mother.

"Joey!" Melissa screamed.

The car was rocking badly now. It was like a nightmare—growling, animal-like teenagers outside, calling his son's name. More windows were broken, and hands reached at them from every direction. The Andersons held each other, panic-stricken. *What do they want with us?* Rich wondered. *What do they want with my son?*

Well, they weren't hard to find, Buffy thought. *Not exactly keeping a low profile.*

The screams and sounds of breaking glass had alerted her from a couple of blocks away, breaking through the suburban stillness like firecrackers in church. Closing in, the roars and snarls of the pack had confirmed her suspicions. She came upon them as they were trying to drag someone from the SUV—probably going for the kid first, as the weakest member, she thought. But the 'rents might be next—neither of them looked all that strong or confident, either.

She jumped into the fray, grabbing the jacket of one of them—she could barely tell which was which, especially since they'd all taken to dressing in the same dark colors—and hurling him to the ground. *Or her,* she corrected.

Then she jumped to the top of the vehicle. Kyle met her up there. She kicked him in the jaw and he sailed off.

Through the smashed-in sunroof, she saw Xander, half in and half out of a window.

"Didn't your Mom teach you?" she asked. "Don't play with your food!"

He slid from the car, facing her. She looked down on him from her rooftop perch. The others backed him up.

"Come on," Buffy said. "You know what you want."

She jumped from the car, on the opposite side from them, and ran. Behind her, she heard their awful hyena laughter. And the unmistakable sounds of them giving chase.

They were coming.

* * *

The zoo was dark and quiet when they arrived. The zookeeper had left Giles's name at the front gate, and the one guard on duty looked too sleepy, or otherwise uninspired, to quiz them too much on their errand. He'd tried to hand them a map showing how to get to the zookeeper's office, but Willow had told the man they'd been there before and knew how to find it. The guard said something about how dark the paths were, but she showed him the big flashlight she'd carried with her from Giles's car. The guard stopped talking.

Of course, the zookeeper's office wasn't their real destination.

The hyenas were.

Within a couple of minutes, they were there. She could smell the sharp musk from outside the enclosure.

"The pathway to the hyena pit," Willow said, winded. "Where's the zookeeper?"

"He must be inside," Giles said, ducking under the yellow tape. "I'll go in and prepare things. You just warn us when you hear Buffy and the others approaching."

He went down the pathway, and was swallowed by the dark. Willow gripped her flashlight a little tighter.

Surrounding the zoo grounds, there was a wide swath of thick vegetation—*Jungle-like, really,* Buffy thought. She ran through it, shoving aside huge hanging leaves, dodging tree trunks. She guessed the idea was that the jungle reduced the animal sounds, for those outside the zoo, and maybe made the noise from Sunnydale more bearable for the animals.

Not that Sunnydale was a really noisy place. But every now and then there were sirens, or demons howling, or hyena-possessed teenagers jumping on cars.

So the soundproofing thing was probably all good.

Except for the part where she was running through the trees and brush, and the hyena kids were running behind her. Chasing her.

Because one thing hyenas knew how to do better than Slayers did was run through the brush. More practice.

She was making good time. They were making better, judging by the leaves and underbrush crashing behind her.

She just hoped her lead would hold until she got them where they needed to be.

Giles walked down the pathway. It was quiet inside, and dark, and a bit rank. There was more tape across the entryway. He wasn't sure exactly what he'd been expecting, but he knew one thing. This wasn't it.

"Doctor . . . ?" he tried. "Zookeeper—?"

A scuffling sound caught his attention and he turned. The zookeeper had come in behind him, from another entrance, possibly.

Only he wasn't dressed like any zookeeper Giles had ever seen.

"Oh, of course," he said. "You're in the Masai ceremonial garb. Are you otherwise prepared for the trans-possession?"

The zookeeper stepped into the glow from lights inside the hyena enclosure. His face was painted blue and white, in a bizarre pattern that Giles half-recognized from the texts he'd pored over in the last few hours. A robe, of a fabric that exactly matched the blue of his face, covered his body, and beneath that he wore some kind of tights. At one ankle and one wrist he wore bone bracelets. He carried a big stick, a staff or club of some kind, which he tossed from hand to hand.

The whole ensemble was more than a little disquieting.

"Almost," the man said.

Giles noticed the strange red markings on the floor. "Right," he said. "The sacred circle. You'd need that to . . ." He was suddenly confused. "Well, this would be here when the children first came. Why would you . . ."

It dawned on him, all at once. He gave a small laugh, and turned to face the fright-masked zookeeper.

"How terribly frustrating for you," Giles said, "that a bunch of schoolchildren could accomplish what you could not."

The zookeeper held his gaze. "It bothered me," he said, matter of factly. "But the power will be mine."

Giles knew, finally, that the man was beyond hope of reasoning. He needed to get away, to warn Willow and Buffy before it was too late. He started to bolt.

But the zookeeper was faster. He stepped in, swinging the club one-handed into Giles's stomach. Giles doubled over, and the blue man whipped the club around, brought it down on the back of Giles's head. Giles went down, unconscious on the floor amid the strange symbols painted there.

The zookeeper didn't waste any time. He grabbed the librarian's ankles and dragged him out of sight. His plans were coming to a head—the last thing he needed was a spare corpse on what was to be the stage for the greatest moment of his life.

They were closer than ever. Buffy could hear them breathing, behind her. Not even panting with the exertion, which, she had to admit, was getting to be a bit of a strain on her.

What was worse, was, they were laughing.

That hysterical half-insane, high-pitched hyena laughter.

Ever closer.

She ran harder.

Willow heard the crashing as they came nearer. It had to be Buffy—not like anyone else would be doing the jogging-for-health thing in the middle of the night in a closed zoo.

Giles had said to warn them, so she passed under the tape and ran down the walk to the hyena house.

"They're almost here!" she called. "Giles . . . ?" No answer. "Giles?"

No Giles, either. The only one there was the zookeeper, and he looked weird, all in blue with his face painted. But Willow was used to weird-looking creatures—at least this guy was human. "Where are the hyenas for the transpossession?" she asked him.

He cocked a thumb over his shoulder, gesturing to the cage. "They're right here, in the feeding area. Stay clear," he warned. "They haven't been fed."

"Where's Giles?"

"He's laying in wait."

"They're almost here," Willow said, fighting hard to keep the panic from her voice. "Shouldn't you bring the hyenas out?"

The zookeeper picked up a long strip of leather. "When the time is right," he said. He grabbed Willow's wrists, started wrapping the leather around them. "I'm gonna need your help."

Well, it had seemed like a good idea at the time.

But now the pack was right on her tail, and Buffy wasn't quite to the hyena house, and if even one of those possessed kids had the presence of mind to make a leap, they could probably catch her.

She'd wrestled Xander. She knew how strong they were. If they brought her down, as a pack, they'd take her. Just like she was one of those antelopes or whatever that they were brunching on in the tapes Willow was watching.

She was close, though. Maybe Giles and Willow could do something.

Like, bury whatever scraps the pack left behind.

She burst through the yellow tape. "They're right behind me!" she called.

Please, Giles, she thought. *Be listening for once, and not talking.*

"That's Buffy! Get ready!" Willow said.

The zookeeper had tied her wrists tightly together with his strap. Now he pulled something from beneath the flowing blue robe he wore—a long knife with a very shiny blade.

"Here," he said, like he was giving her a present.

"What is this?"

"The predatory act, remember?" he replied. He moved behind her, holding her in one arm and bringing the knife to her throat.

"Oh, right," Willow said. Talking was hard with the blade pressed against her skin. "You'll pretend to slash my throat and put the evil in the hyenas?"

He looked her in the eyes, but there was nothing reassuring in his voice. "Something like that."

It was clear now that he wasn't kidding. Nor was he on their side.

Buffy burst into the hyena house. There was a strange-looking, blue-garbed man holding a knife to Willow's neck. And Will's hands were tied. There was no sign of Giles. Just to make things more complicated, Willow shouted, "Buffy! It's a trap!"

Buffy stopped in her tracks.

Which, come to think of it, might not have been the best idea, since the pack was still running full speed behind her.

Xander plowed into her, throwing one arm around her midriff and driving her to the ground. Then the others were on her, hands tearing at her, teeth gnashing hungrily.

"Nyumba Ya Sanaa!" the zookeeper called. She recognized the edge in his voice from the first time he'd spoken to them outside the enclosure, and realized that's who the blue guy was.

Everybody looked at him. Except Buffy, who, because the pack wasn't looking at her, looked at them.

Their eyes, after all, were glowing green. It was the kind of thing that caught your attention.

All of them—Kyle, Heidi, Tor, Rhonda—eyes flashing like traffic lights saying go. She risked a glance at the zookeeper, and his eyes flashed the same weird glow, as if in response to them.

And she suddenly understood what it meant. This whole thing had been a setup. Somehow the hyena spirit had accidentally gone into Xander and the rest, when this guy actually wanted it for himself. So he'd arranged for everyone to be brought back here when he was ready.

Now the hyena was out of the kids, and concentrated in one man. Who wanted it there.

He was going to be trouble.

As if forgetting how to use tools, the zookeeper dropped his knife, grabbing Willow's head between his hands. He roared like a wild beast. He leaned toward her, baring his teeth like he meant to rip into her flesh.

"Willow!" It was Xander. Sounding like himself. She never thought his voice could sound so wonderful. He pushed away from Buffy, launched himself across the room, and slammed into the growling zookeeper. They both went down, but the zookeeper regained his footing quickly. When Xander came at him again, he swung a backhanded blow that knocked the teen to one side.

With Xander off her, however, and the rest of the pack watching the fight, Buffy could stand. She did, then launched a kick at the zookeeper's painted jaw. She connected, hard, and he fell back. In a second he was up again, and charging her. She stopped him for a moment with a left, and when he attacked again, she grabbed his robes and used his own momentum to throw him over her shoulder and down onto the hard stone floor.

He was powerful, though. Most men would have been out cold, but he jumped up and came back for more with an animal-like growl.

So she used the same trick, in the other direction. Grasping his robes, turning, spinning, bringing him over her shoulder and down.

Except that this time, because he was coming at her from the other way, "down" meant into the hyena pit.

He screamed.

He reappeared again a moment later, trying to haul himself out by the bars of the cage. But there was a ferocious growling behind him. He screamed again, in pain this time more than fear, and was dragged down from the bars.

He was out of sight, but the growling continued. And even worse, crunching, gnawing, gnashing of teeth.

Buffy caught a glimpse of Kyle and his friends as they

ran out of the hyena house, horrified. She didn't blame them.

She took another last look inside the cage and was sorry she had. If the zookeepers had rules against feeding the animals, she was sure feeding the zookeepers to the animals must be an even worse violation.

When she turned away, unsteady and a little queasy, she saw Xander—who looked, at last, like the plain old Xander everyone knew and loved—untying Willow's hands.

A door opened, and Giles staggered into the room. He put a hand to his glasses, trying to gain his balance. "Uh," he said. "Did I miss anything?"

Where does a girl start?

The next day was one of those bright, sunny days when it really becomes clear that summer is just around the corner. Buffy, Willow, and Xander walked across the quad, heading for class. Buffy was enjoying the sunshine, and, strange as it seemed, enjoying being with Xander.

"I heard the vice principal is taking over until they can find a replacement," Will said.

"It shouldn't be hard to find a new principal," Buffy said. "Unless they ask what happened to the last one."

"Okay, but I had nothing to do with that, right?" Xander asked for the millionth time.

"Right," Buffy agreed.

They started up an outside staircase. "You only ate the pig," Willow added.

"I ate a pig? Was he cooked and called 'bacon,' or . . ." Xander put his hand to his forehead, in obvious dismay. "Oh my God. I ate a pig? I mean, the whole trichinosis issue aside, yuck."

"Well, it wasn't really you," Buffy assured him.

"Well, I remember going on the field trip, and then going down in the hyena house," Xander said. "Next thing some guy's holding Willow and he's got a knife."

"You saved my life," Willow said.

"Hey." Xander stopped at the top of the stairs. "Nobody messes with my Willow." He put his arms around her, drew her into a hug.

She wasn't, Buffy noted, in any hurry to break it off.

"This is definitely the superior Xander," Buffy announced. "Accept no substitutes."

Xander touched his lips, his chest. Buffy thought he was maybe going a little overboard on the hand language, but, in comparison to the hyena bit, decided it was not worth getting worked up over. "I didn't do anything else, did I? Around you guys? Anything embarrassing?"

"Naah," she assured him.

"Not at all," Willow added.

Buffy took Willow by the hand. "Come on," she said. "We're gonna be late."

Willow looked at Xander. "See you at lunch."

"Cool," he replied. "Hey, going vegetarian, huh?" He gave them a broad smile and two thumbs-up.

He was pretty sure they were buying it.

Good.

It felt great to be himself again. He preferred that, he realized. *But sometimes, you have to pretend a little, keep your own secrets. For the sake of your friends.*

He turned and walked a few steps—straight toward Giles, who was coming right for him, looking crisp in a fresh suit and tie.

"I've been reading up on my animal possession,"

Giles said, "and I cannot find anything anywhere about memory loss afterward."

"Did you tell them that?" Xander pointed toward the girls.

Giles leaned close to his ear. "Your secret dies with me," he said.

That should have been enough. Except Giles knew. And he knew Giles knew. It might be better to let Buffy know, than Giles. He could trust the man, he was sure of that. *But still . . .*

"Shoot me, stuff me, mount me," Xander said.

Giles clapped him on the shoulder. Co-conspirators to the end. Xander walked away from him, hands on top of his head, as embarrassed as he could remember ever having been.

There was a bright side to this, he knew.

He just didn't have the slightest idea what it was.

The closest he could get to it was that things could not possibly get worse. Not all that bright, after all. He was sure that if he could get over feeling so mortified, he'd be able to find a better one.

The "if" thing.

He went to class.

INTERLUDE

Xander continued heading out of town. The wind rushed past him, the black strip of road appeared magically beneath his headlights. He'd left the zoo far behind, and had an actual destination in mind now.

He gave the car its head, steering with the lightest touch possible on the wheel. It was almost like the car knew where they were going.

After another few minutes, he could smell salt-water in the air.

Much had changed since his little adventure as part of the canine family. He'd heard theories that the rate of change accelerated with every passing year—that the difference in the way people lived between, say, the year 500 and the year 1500 was not huge. But in recent times, things had been advancing at amazing rates. The people who were alive in 1800 would barely have recognized the world of 1900, and would have been totally dumfounded by the time 2000 came around.

Anyway, that business with the hyena spirits had been sophomore year. He'd been young and foolish then. As he matured, he knew the changes in his life, the various transformations that a man went through as he grew older, would be more subtle, but ultimately more defining.

And, he hoped, they would have less to do with canines of any kind.

When Buffy showed up in town and everything changed, Xander realized that Sunnydale—and his life—had seemed pretty constant, unchanging, before. All those years of peace and quiet, growing up in an idyllic seaside town, and then . . .

And then things got interesting. And frightening.

The worst was when Buffy died.

She had, literally, been clinically dead, he knew. If she hadn't, then Kendra, the new Slayer, wouldn't have been activated. But she was, and that meant that Buffy's close call had been a little more than just close.

Xander had been there for her that time, though. He had administered mouth to mouth—which he still thought about with a degree of enjoyment from time to time. Angel stood helplessly by, watching, while Xander breathed life-giving air into her lungs. And she had come back.

There had been so many other things, happy and sad, momentous and tiny. Buffy had fallen deeply in love with Angel, and then been terribly hurt when he turned bad again, after having been good for so many years. That whole good vampire business, it turned out, had been the result of a gypsy's curse that restored the vampire's soul—and therefore, his conscience—to him.

Stricken with guilt over the things he'd done in the intervening years, Angel had tried to live as one of the good guys, battling vampire nasties whenever he could. That was the Angel Buffy had fallen for.

Unfortunately for that relationship, the curse was lifted. Soulless again, Angel flipflopped back into fangs and forehead guy. He killed Miss Calendar, who was Giles's girlfriend and a member of the same gypsy tribe that had cursed him. And Buffy vowed to take him out.

Xander pulled the car to a stop in the parking lot by the beach. He jumped out, not bothering with the door. From this spot, he could hear the roar of the surf, but he could barely see the water.

He hiked down the path, to the wide stretch of beach. There it was, a vast carpet of black, spreading before him like velvet on which someone had scattered a handful of diamonds: the full moon's shimmering reflection on the water.

Things had been quite different for him, as well. Such as, dating Cordelia Chase. That had come as a shock to both of them—a surprise that wasn't entirely pleasant, but far from all bad. It had started with an innocent kiss—okay, not *so* innocent, but still. Then it grew into an illicit affair, kept secret from everyone in the school. Finally, the truth had come out, and people grew to accept it. Even Willow.

Although it was probably easier for Willow to accept now that she had Oz, rock guitarist and teen werewolf, who did the whole Michael Landon routine at every full moon.

And dating Cordelia had, at least, proven more pleasant and satisfying than his short-lived romance with Ampata, who turned out to be an ancient Incan mummy, reanimated and ravenous.

The slaying gig had become more complicated, too. Buffy had killed the Master, but the Anointed One had been around to make things difficult for her. Until Spike and Drusilla came to town, and Spike killed the Anointed One. Between Spike, Drusilla, and the newly evil Angel, the ranks of local vampires had become very dangerous indeed.

Xander kicked his shoes off, removed his socks, and pushed his toes into the cold sand. He stuffed the socks into his shoes and carried them down to where the waves scoured the sand smooth and hard, let the frigid water wash up around his feet. *For a California guy,* he realized, *I don't spend a lot of time in the ocean.*

And that, suddenly, brought back a whole new set of memories. He backed away from the water, hurried back up to the parking lot. There he stamped his feet on the pavement to shake the sand off. Leaning against the car, he tugged his socks back on, then his shoes. He tied them and got back behind the wheel.

He felt better now. From this vantage point, the ocean looked calm and safe.

And distant.

The way he liked it.

Chapter 6

There was nothing tropical about the beach that night. *Or even subtropical,* Xander thought. *Downright cold is more like it.*

Trouble was, he seemed to be the only one who felt that way. Everywhere he looked, kids were having fun, dancing and talking and generally carrying on.

Okay, they were dressed in sweaters and jackets and huddled around bonfires. But still, they seemed to be enjoying themselves despite the elements.

Sunnydale High's athletes weren't exactly on a first-name basis with victory parties, so maybe the concept of holding them in comfortable surroundings was still unfamiliar to them.

"All I'm saying is, it was a stupid idea to have a victory party at the beach," Xander said, warming his palms over a fire. He wore a striped sweater over a T-shirt, but that wasn't nearly enough. "It's officially nippy. So say my nips."

Cordelia, who was here more or less as his date, and his longtime best bud Willow stood at the fire with him.

"I think it's festive," Willow said. "It's a party with nature."

"Well, it's the team's choice," Cordelia added. "It was their victory."

"Team? Swim team." Xander chuckled. "Hardly what I call a team. The Yankees . . . Abbott and Costello . . . the A . . . Now those were teams."

"Jealous?" Cordy asked.

"No," Xander replied. He reflected further. "Yes. But no more than yes. I mean, look at that." He indicated a student partway across the beach—tall and muscular, with close-shaven hair, wearing only a Hawaiian shirt in spite of temperatures that Xander considered arctic.

"Dodd McAlvy," he went on. "Last month he's the freak with jicama breath who waxes his back. He wins a few meets and suddenly he inherits the 'cool' gene?"

"Well, all I know is, my cheerleading squad's wasted a lot of pep on losers," Cordelia argued. "It's about time our school excelled at something."

"You're forgetting our high mortality rate," Willow offered.

"We're number one!" Xander shouted. *Leave it to Willow to find the cogent argument.* Xander did a slow turn, but the students around him seemed oblivious to his sudden display of school spirit. *Or,* he thought morbidly, *school spirits.*

Perched on a rock by the water's edge, Buffy studied the moon's silver reflection on the dark water of the

Pacific Ocean. The leather jacket Angel had given her kept most of the chill off. She still wore it, even though . . . well, even though.

The party roared around her, as oblivious to her presence as the creatures at the bottom of this sea were to the chunk of rock that orbited high above. But like those creatures and the moon, every student here had been touched in some way by Buffy. If it weren't for her, the Hellmouth would be a far more dangerous place than it was.

And it was pretty bad, even with her around.

They never even know the danger they're in, she thought. And that's how she wanted to keep it. Even though it also meant that they never knew her contribution toward keeping them from harm's way.

"Beautiful," a voice from behind her said. "Isn't it?"

Cameron Walker. She knew him, of course, but not at all well. He was a member of the swim team—one of the best swimmers, from what she'd heard. *He's also good looking,* she thought. Tall, powerfully built, with an easy smile and curly brown hair instead of the shaved look favored by some of the swim team. No Angel, maybe. *But then, who is?* And besides, Angel was evil now, while Cam was just a jock. And Angel, soulless or not, was still a vampire. *Maybe a normal guy is just what I need, to give me a little break from the slaying and all.*

"Yeah," she began. "It's just so—"

He cut her off, and went on, staring out at the sparkling surface. "Eternal. Our true mother giving birth to new life, and devouring old." He moved around and sat on the rock, next to Buffy. When he continued, he was looking at her, not at the sea. "Always adaptable and nurturing, yet constant and timeless."

"Boy," Buffy said, surprised at such poetic language coming from someone she had always seen as just another athlete. "I was just gonna go with 'big' and 'wet.' "

Cameron gave a polite laugh. "Me and some of the other guys on the team, we come out once a week to train in it. See, we swim against the current."

"Funny, that's how I feel most of the time," Buffy said. She turned to him and used her best sportscaster voice. "So, Cameron Walker. You've just won the state semifinals. What are you gonna do next?"

"I'm going to hang out with Buffy Summers," he replied. "Get to know her."

Whoa. That's no "I'm going to Disneyland," she thought.

"Hey, pause that tape for a second," she said.

"No pressure," Cameron said, clearly trying to put her at ease. "I just like being around you, that's all."

It almost worked. She looked at his face for a moment, his all-American good looks, and then turned away, toward the sea. Considering.

"Somebody help me!" she heard. Back from the thick of the party. The voice carried an edge of genuine panic, and the Slayer was instantly on her guard.

Up the beach, she saw Dodd McAlvy holding another student's head into one of the big stainless-steel tubs filled with ice to keep the drinks cold. The student had a red sweatshirt on, but Buffy couldn't make out his face until Dodd let him up for air. It was Jonathon Levenson, one of those brainy kids who were never quite smart enough to avoid becoming someone's target. He came up gasping and choking.

"C'mon, Jonny," Dodd shouted. He knew he was performing for an audience. "You gotta hold your breath longer than that if you ever want to make the team. Hey, somebody time him!" He shoved Jonathon back into the ice-cold water.

Buffy made her move. She came up behind Dodd, caught hold of his shirt, and yanked him backward, off Jonathon.

"Hey!" Dodd shouted.

Tugging on Dodd's shirt drew his sleeve back, and revealed a tattoo Buffy hadn't seen before on his upper arm—a shark with an insane grin, front fins drawn into tight fists, a cigar clenched between his teeth.

"Nice tat," Buffy said. "What, they ran out of Tweety Bird?" She gave him a shove and he went face-first into the sand.

"Hey, what's your problem?" Dodd asked.

"Had it coming to you, bro," Cameron said, a broad smile on his face. He stood behind Buffy, backing her play.

Dodd regained his feet and started to step toward Buffy and Cameron like he wanted to continue the altercation. Before he could, though, he was intercepted by another swimmer, Gage Petronzi.

"Chill, dude," Gage said. He was even taller than Dodd, wearing a high turtleneck sweater that accentuated his total skinhead cut. "A bunch of us are gonna take a little night dip down the beach. You in?"

"Whatever," Dodd said. He shot Buffy a "die, freak" look, then allowed himself to be led away.

Buffy turned to Jonathon, still dripping wet and shivering in the brisk night air. "Hey," she said. "Let's get you a towel."

"Why don't you mind your own business?" Jonathon shot back. "I can handle this without your help." He stormed off, angry—misplaced anger, Buffy thought. It should have been directed at Dodd, not at her. *But there you go. People.*

It was almost enough to make a girl prefer being with some other form of life. *Like, say, vampires.*

"See," she said to Cameron. "It's fun to hang out with me."

Heading down the beach toward the surf, Gage said, "Man, I can't believe Buffy."

"Man, that girl gives me the creeps," Dodd agreed. He took a few more steps toward the water's edge, and then stopped. The waves rolled in and pulled away, and he felt something. A tugging, deep inside him. An urge to become . . .

Gage had gone on ahead. Suddenly, he became aware of an odor—no, call it what it was, a stench—ripping at his nostrils like poisoned fishhooks.

"Ahh, dude," he said, making a face. "What is that foulness?"

He looked back to where Dodd had been, but his friend was no longer in sight.

"Hey, Dodd!" he called, turning a three-sixty. No sign of him. He had just been right here . . . "Dude!" No reply. He gave a shrug and jogged off toward another group of partyers, farther down the beach.

The roar of the surf, this close to the water, drowned out the screams and the wet, tearing noise. And in the dark, Gage missed entirely the pile of tattered clothing and something else, soft and glistening red in the moonlight, still steaming in the cold night air. Had he seen it, and gone close enough, he would have seen a familiar Hawaiian shirt mixed in with the other, messier bits. And closer still, he might have seen the decoration on one of the flat surfaces—a tattoo of a grinning, two-fisted shark, chomping on a stogie.

But he didn't see any of that, nor did he see, not so far away, the shadow of a figure dashing into the opening of a large water pipe. The pipe carried water to the sea, and it led away from the beach.

Toward Sunnydale.

CHAPTER 7

"Okay, good pie charts, everyone," Willow said. She walked up and down between the rows of desks, looking at the screens of the students' computers. She really enjoyed this student teaching thing she'd been asked to do.

Enjoyed it almost as much as she hated the reason she'd been asked to do it. Willow was replacing Miss Calendar, who had been murdered by Angel. She thought she'd never forgive Angel for that, and remembering the teacher made Willow almost regret the teaching gig altogether.

But not completely.

"Good," she said as she passed their desks. "All good."

"Thanks," one of the kids said. "*Kids,*" she thought. *As if I'm any older than they are.*

"Nice, " she said to another.

And then there was Gage.

Toward the back of the class she risked a glance at Gage Petronzi's screen. *He may be a great swimmer,* she thought, *but his computer skills leave a little something to be desired.* Like, if he could swing a job at the supermarket, he'd better plan to be a bagger rather than a checker. The concept of using technology for good instead of evil seemed to be beyond him.

"Gage, your pie chart is looking a lot like solitaire," Willow said. She leaned closer, took a better look. "With naked ladies on the cards."

"What's your point?" Gage asked.

"No point."

The bell rang. Chairs scuffed back across the floor, students gathered books and headed for the door. Gage moved with them, as if he couldn't wait to get out of class.

Principal Snyder, Mr. Flutie's replacement, pushed inside the classroom door as the students went out. He was short, almost elfin, with a wide, balding head. His gray suit was three-piece, both vest and jacket buttoned.

He met Gage just inside the doorway. "Nice work in yesterday's meet, son," he said. "Now let's go for it."

Gage went around him, out of the room. Willow hesitantly approached the principal.

"Uh, hi there," she said. Then added, "Sir."

"Rosenberg," he said. "How's the class? Everything in order?"

"Well, actually—"

"Great," he interrupted. "I've been talking to the board. We've been having trouble finding a competent teacher this late in the term. Do you think you can continue subbing through finals?"

Willow could feel her face breaking into a wide smile.

It was so good to be appreciated for the job she was doing. "Oh, sure. I like teaching."

"Isn't that nice," Mr. Snyder said without a trace of sincerity. "You're a team player and I like that. A team player wants everyone on the team to succeed. Wants everyone to pass."

"Uh, yeah, sure." Willow was uncertain where this was going, and uncomfortable with getting there.

"I understand there's a problem with Gage Petronzi."

Vast relief. "Oh, good, then you know. Well, yeah," she said. "Besides the behavior problem, he won't do homework, and his test scores are, well, actually he doesn't have any test scores since he never shows up when we have—"

"I'm not interested in any of that," the principal interrupted again. This was looking like a trend. Or maybe a habit. "I'm interested in why," he went on, his voice stern, "when this school is on the brink of winning its first state championship in fifteen years, you slap a crucial member of that team with a failing grade that would force his removal. Is this how you show your school spirit?"

"Yes," Willow said. "Well, I mean, no. I mean, I'm just trying to grade fairly."

"Gage is a champion," Mr. Snyder insisted. "He's under more pressure than the other students. And *I* think we need to cut him some slack." He headed for the door.

Now she knew where the conversation had been going, beyond any doubt. And she didn't like it. "You're asking me to change his grade?"

He stopped in his track, swiveled, came back into the room. "I never said any such thing," he said. His voice was low and deliberate. He stopped directly in front of Willow, almost as if staring her down, or daring her to flinch. "All I'm suggesting is that you recheck your figures. And I think you'll find a grade more fitting to an athlete of Gage's stature. Perhaps something in a 'D.' "

He left Willow alone in the classroom, her good mood shattered.

Xander could barely believe what Willow was saying. Actually, he could believe it—Principal Snyder had been around long enough to make his contempt for anyone under the age of thirty well known, that Xander could believe just about anything. But still . . .

"Just like that?" he asked. "He actually told you to alter his grade?"

They were coming down from the second floor, Cordelia between them, he and Willow flanking her. Cordy looked, he had to say, terrific in a very short black skirt with a sleeveless white sweater, a couple of black stripes around her midriff.

"Exactly," Willow replied, bringing his attention back to the subject at hand. "Except for actually telling me to. But he made it perfectly clear what he wasn't telling me."

They hit the first floor, made a right turn, headed toward class. "That is wrong," Xander declared. "Big, fat, spanking wrong. It's a slap in the face to every one of us that studied hard and worked long hours to earn our Ds."

Cordelia contributed her own brand of uplifting dialogue to the conversation. "Xander, I know you take pride in being the voice of the common wuss, but the truth is certain people are entitled to special privileges. They're called winners. That's the way the world works."

He tried to ignore the fact that the girl speaking was also the one he was dating. After all, she was still

Cordelia, even if they both had experienced sudden, and recurring, losses of judgment. "And what about that nutty 'all men are created equal' thing?"

"Propaganda spouted out by the ugly and less deserving."

"I think that was Lincoln," Xander offered.

"Disgusting mole and stupid hat," Cordy said.

"Actually," Willow pointed out, "it was Jefferson."

"Kept slaves, remember?"

Xander was a little surprised by Cordelia's grasp of American history, but kept that to himself. "You know what really grates my cheese?" he asked. "That Buffy's not here to share my moral outrage about swim team perks. She's too busy being *one* of them."

Cameron Walker's midnight blue Ford Mustang pulled into the school parking lot. Lunch with Cam off-campus had been—well, "interesting" wasn't exactly the word for it, because it wasn't. Or, he wasn't. *Maybe "enlightening,"* she thought, her mind wandering.

"I don't know, a dolphin," Cameron was saying. Rather, continuing to say, since he had been talking nonstop for basically the entire lunch period. And the thing of it was, she couldn't remember a single thing he had said. "A dolphin in the ocean. Because, you know, when I'm in the vastness of the ocean, it's like I'm never alone. You ever hear of a woman named Gertrude Ederle?"

"No. No, I can't say that I have, Cam."

Her response was pretty much just an opportunity for him to draw a breath. He didn't actually listen to her. She felt her eyelids getting heavy as he droned on. "First woman to swim the English Channel. Same thing. She would talk to it. She'd carry on entire conversations with it. Sometimes I do that. Once I was out—"

"Listen, Cam." She interrupted him, fearing for her sanity if he went on any longer. "Thanks again. I'd forgotten how nice it is to just talk . . . or in my case, listen, without any romantic pressure."

"Hey, I'm not about pressure," he said. "I just want you comfortable."

"I'm comfy," she said. "I'm so comfy I'm nodding off, actually. Which is why—"

His turn to interrupt. "Are you wearing a bra?" His gaze roamed down the front of her sleeveless top.

What? she thought. "What?"

"C'mon," Cameron said. "I mean, tell me you haven't been thinking about this ever since last night."

Buffy reached for the door handle. "What I'm thinking about is that I should probably get out of here."

But Cameron knew the car better than she did, and he punched the electronic door lock button before she got her door open. The locks chunked shut. Her handle didn't work.

"Relax," he said. "I'm not going to hurt you."

Well, duh. She knew that. She was the Slayer, after all. If being killed by the Master didn't slow her down, an eager swimmer didn't have much chance against her. "Oh, it's not me I'm worried about."

Cam, though, seemed to like the sound of that. "You like it rough," he said, reaching for her.

She caught the reaching arm, yanked it forward to pull him off balance. With her other hand she grabbed the hair on the back of his head, slamming him back against his seat, and then driving his face forward into the steering wheel. The horn honked as Cam's honker hammered it.

"Ow!" he screeched. "Oh, you broke my nose!"

Just then she noticed, as Cameron held his face in his

hands and moaned, Principal Snyder looking into the car. "Unhappy" was the kindest word she could think of for his expression. He gave her the universal "come here" finger wag, except that in this case it was more of a "come here and meet six weeks of detention" gesture.

Later, in Nurse Greenleigh's office, the stocky woman prepared an ice pack for Cam's nose. Prepared in the sense of slamming it down on a countertop with enough force to sound like a small explosion. She put the ice pack on Cameron's face, and he flinched. There was already a bandage wrapped around his wrist.

Buffy was too concerned with defending herself to care much about what he was going through.

"I wasn't the attacker, Principal Snyder," she said. "I was the attacked."

"That's not how it looked from where I was standing."

"I don't know what happened," Cameron added helpfully. "I mean, first she leads me on, then she goes schizo on me."

"Lead you on?" Buffy asked, astonished. *Does he really believe—?* "When did I lead you on?"

"C'mon," he said, more to Mr. Snyder than to her. "I mean, look at the way she dresses."

Which wasn't, she thought, really so bad, was it? A reasonably tight—but not excessively so—sleeveless black V-neck top, a short white skirt, black boots. *What's wrong with this?*

The door opened and another visitor entered the crowded nurse's office. Coach Marin, the swim coach. He was a big, sturdy man, white-haired, clad all in Sunnydale High burgundy and gold. *School spirit personified,* she thought. *Our first winning coach in years. Come to soothe his wounded warrior.*

Just what I need.

"Coach," Mr. Snyder said.

The coach pushed past Snyder, approached Cam.

"How we doing, Cameron?" he asked.

Cameron moved the ice pack away, held his nose out for the coach's inspection.

"Coach Marin," Principal Snyder said. "How bad does it look?"

The coach examined Cam's nose like a general inspecting his troops. "Well, luckily, it's not broken. But it sure as hell's gonna sting for a few days."

"I mean, our chance of winning the state championship," the principal said, clarifying his priorities. He drew Coach Marin to one side. "Can we still do it?"

"Oh." Marin said. "I'm gonna need Cam back at a hundred and ten percent. He's the best swimmer I got, now that Dodd . . ." He trailed off.

"What happened to Dodd?" Buffy asked.

"That's none of your concern," Mr. Snyder snapped at her. "You'd better hope that boy's nose heals before the meet this Friday."

Coach Marin left them, went back to where Cam sat on the examining table. "Walker," he said, "I want you to hit the steam room as soon as you're done here. Try to keep those sinuses clear." Turning to Nurse Greenleigh, he added, "You take care of my boy, Ruthie."

"I always do," the nurse replied.

Then Coach Marin addressed Buffy. "And you, try to dress more appropriately from now on. This isn't a dance club." He looked her up and down once, and stalked away. Principal Snyder followed the coach. Cam just sat on the table, the ice pack near his face not quite hiding the big unpleasant grin there.

* * *

"So I'm treated like the baddie," Buffy told her friends. "Just because he has a sprained wrist and a bloody nose, and I don't have a scratch on me. Which, granted, hurts my case a little on the surface. But meanwhile, he gets away with it because he's on the 'aren't we the most' swim team, who, by the way, if no one's noticed, have been acting like real jerks lately . . ."

She slowed her rant long enough to realize that Giles, Willow, and Xander were all looking up at her from their various books. Will was seated behind a table, Giles leaning on it near her, and Xander sat on top of the table, a big book open in his lap. *It looks,* Buffy thought, *more like study hall than the library.* Well, she amended, it actually did look like a library, she just wasn't all that used to it being used as one.

"So," she laughed softly. "Anything new with you guys?" She sat in a chair at the end of the table.

"Thank you for taking an interest," Giles said. As always, his British accent made everything he said sound so, well, English, or something. "Apparently, some remains were found on the beach this morning. Some human remains."

"Dodd McAlvy's remains," Willow added.

"Vampires?" Buffy asked.

"No," Giles replied. "He was eviscerated. Nothing left but skin and cartilage."

"In other words," Xander offered, "this was no boating accident!"

"So, something ripped him open and ate out his insides?" Buffy asked, incredulous.

"Like an Oreo cookie," Willow said. The others looked at her, but no one spoke. "Well," she went on, "except for, you know, without the chocolatey cookie goodness."

"Principal Snyder's asked the faculty to keep the news quiet for now so as not to unduly upset the students," Giles said.

"For 'students,' read 'swim team.' " The sarcasm was evident in Xander's tone.

"So, we're looking for a beastie," Willow explained.

Giles picked up the thread. "That eats humans whole, except for the skin."

"This doesn't make any sense," Buffy said.

"Yeah!" Xander agreed. "The skin's the best part!"

Buffy shrugged, as in, my point exactly. "Any demons with high cholesterol?"

Giles turned and gave her a look.

"You're gonna think about that later, mister, and you're gonna laugh," Buffy said, pointing at him for emphasis.

She hoped it was true.

Cameron Walker sat in the steam room, hunched over, elbows resting on his knees. The warm healing mist soothed his aching muscles, but his nose was still bothering him. He tipped his head back, touched his nose with his fingers, drew them away. No blood. The skin had been broken, but at least the bleeding had been stopped.

He thought he heard a noise, somewhere outside the steam room. He listened. Nothing. He began to relax again—

And the door flew open. Cameron started.

"Okay, son," Coach Marin said. "I think you've had enough. Time to hit the shower." The coach disappeared through the fog.

Night. The school was as close to silent as big buildings ever get. Xander headed down the empty corridor, jingling change in his hand. He was parched, and his eyes were crossing from all the reading they'd been doing. Why wasn't there some kind of Unabridged Demonic Dictionary? "Too much research," he said as he went. "Need beverage."

He was looking at the coins in his palm, counting, so he wasn't looking at the intersecting hallway.

Which was where Cameron Walker was coming from, also not looking. He slammed into Xander, scattering his coins on the floor.

"Hey, watch it," Cam said.

Xander gave Cam an awed expression, as if having encountered royalty. "Oh, forgive me, your swimteamliness." He squatted to pick up his change.

"Loser," Cameron said, continuing on his way.

"Liking the nose, Cam," Xander said. "Good look for you."

Cam stopped, turned back to face Xander. "Meaning what?"

"Meaning Buffy must not be on your list of privileges after all." Cam closed with him, arms crossed over his chest, but Xander held his ground and laughed. "Man, I love it when you guys mess with her."

Cameron shook his head dismissively. "You're lucky I'm hungry."

"Oh, the cafeteria's closed," Xander said, dripping mock sympathy.

"Not to me."

He headed in that direction, leaving Xander standing in the intersection, wondering what it was about swim team members that made them think they were put on the planet for the rest of humanity to serve.

* * *

The cafeteria was dark. Moonlight striped the walls. Warming lights warmed empty stainless steel trays. No food to be seen. Cameron walked through the big room. There would be something around, maybe back in the freezers.

But out here, there was a *nasty* smell. "God, what is that?" he asked no one in particular.

No one answered.

Xander stood before the soda machine, faced with the eternal dilemma. So many choices, only one mouth. "Grape, orange. Orange, grape."

And from the direction of the cafeteria, a bone-shilling scream split the silence.

Soda choices would have to wait. He ran.

The cafeteria looked empty when he got there. Lights off, nobody home.

But somebody had screamed, and Gage had been coming this way. Xander went in.

He noticed, pretty quickly, that tables were upended, chairs scattered. The custodians didn't usually leave the place in this kind of shape. Which meant something had happened.

And, from the smell of the place, that something wasn't in the category of good somethings. The smell was rank. Fetid, even.

He came around one of the overturned tables and saw it. A steaming pile of something, clothing and skin and generally bloody ickiness. Most of it was unrecognizable, but there was a hand that still looked like a hand, five fingers and everything.

Xander felt nauseated. He put a hand over his nose and mouth, both to block out the smell and to keep himself from getting sick. "Oh my God," he said. "Oh God."

He had to get help. *Buffy and the others are in the library,* he thought. *I could be there in less than a minute, if I left right now. Especially if I run.*

Running was definitely in the plan.

He turned to do just that, but then he didn't.

Because when he turned, he found himself face-to-face with a monster from his worst nightmares.

It was green and covered in scales. It had teeth, lots of teeth, and hanging down beside its horrible open mouth were whiskers, fish whiskers like a catfish has, which is the reason it's called a catfish, otherwise looking nothing like a cat. Its hands ended in fingers with big claws on them. It stood almost a head taller than him.

It screamed.

So did Xander.

Chapter 8

Cordelia, it turned out, could sort of draw. Which, who knew? Xander had thought her skills were limited to cheerleading, cutting sarcasm, and personal grooming. But there she sat, sketchpad on her lap, pencil in her hand, sketching out a creature that bore some resemblance to the thing he had encountered in the cafeteria.

Emphasis on "some" resemblance.

"No, the mouth's a lot bigger," he said. "And downward. Like this." He demonstrated, turning his own mouth down. "With more teeth."

She dropped the pad and pencil down on the table and stood, impatience in her voice. "I'm doing the best I can."

"Is that what you saw, Xander?" Giles asked, trying to defuse things.

"Yeah. I think so. Pretty much."

Giles drew the next part out. Giving Xander time to decide, yes or no. "Are you sure?"

"Well, it was dark. And the thing went through the window so quick. And I was a little shocked when I saw it and . . ."

"Go ahead, say it," Cordy prompted. "You ran like a woman." *That biting sarcasm talent, coming through again.*

"Hey," Xander protested. "If you saw this thing you'd run like a woman, too."

The library door swung open, and Buffy and Willow came in.

"Buffy was right," Will announced. "According to statistics, Dodd and Cameron were the best swimmers on the team." She handed Giles a computer printout.

"First and second, actually," Buffy put in. "Which means, if my theory's correct, that Gage Petronzi, the third best swimmer on the team, would be the next item on the menu."

"God, this is so sad," Cordelia said. Xander was surprised. *A touch of humanity?* "We're never going to win the state championship," she continued. *False alarm.* "I think I've lost all will to cheerlead."

Xander lifted one hand into the air. "Raise your hand if you feel her pain."

Giles ignored them both, studying the printout. "If you're saying these killings aren't random," he said, "it would suggest someone's out for revenge."

"And raise the possibility that someone brought forth this sea demon from whence it came to exact that revenge," Buffy said. Then, as if hearing her own words for the first time, she looked at Giles and added, " 'from whence it came?' I'm spending way too much time around you."

"Who would hate the swim team that much, though?" Xander asked. "Besides me, I mean."

Willow had a thought, which she expressed by raising her hand and saying, "Ooo."

Buffy encouraged her. "Willow?"

"Jonathon! He was bullied by Dodd the other day on the beach, remember?"

"He did say he could take care of things himself," Buffy said. "It's a good call, Will. You should question him."

Willow was a little taken aback, but smiled quickly. "Really? Me?" she asked, then got into it. "I'll crack him like an egg."

"Meanwhile," Giles said, his over-the-glasses gaze landing on Buffy, "I think swimmer number three might benefit from your watchful eye and protection. Discreetly, of course."

"I'm on it," Buffy said.

"What about me?" Xander asked. "What can I do?"

"Well," Cordelia said. "You could go out to the parking lot and practice running like a man."

Xander folded his arms over his chest, defensively. There were some things she was just *too* good at.

Gage Petronzi sat in the student lounge, feet up on a table, his attention riveted to a handheld video game.

Or so Buffy hoped.

It was the next day, and the lounge was full of students. But it wasn't so full that he wouldn't be able to see her sitting there, if he looked up. She was not exactly inconspicuous in her bright purple shirt and black pants. She held a magazine in front of her face, flipping pages now and then to make it look like she was reading it. But mostly, she watched Gage. The last thing she needed was for one of those creatures to snatch him right out from under her.

He looked up. She turned away quickly, locking her gaze on the magazine. When she thought it was safe, she snuck another glance his way.

The interrogation took place in Willow's computer classroom. She had Jonathon sitting in the front row, her gooseneck desk lamp turned and aimed into his eyes. She'd seen enough movies to know how this worked. Even *Basic Instinct,* but then, she thought, that didn't really apply in this case.

"So, Jonathon," she said, in her best interrogative voice. "You tried out for the swim team twice and never made it?"

"I'm asthmatic," he replied simply. "I couldn't keep up."

"You resented it, didn't you?"

"Maybe."

"You hated being pushed around by Dodd and the others." *And who wouldn't?* she thought.

"So?"

For a moment, she thought he had her there. But then she pulled it out. "So, you wanted revenge, didn't you?" And again, louder, right in his face. "Didn't you?"

This was the part where they always broke down and confessed.

Jonathon blinked back tears. "Yeah, okay? I did!"

Success.

No rubber hoses even necessary.

This grilling thing is easier than it looks.

"So," she went on. "You delved into the black arts and conjured up a beast from the ocean's depths to wreak your vengeance."

He looked at her like she had gone insane.

Alexander LaVelle Harris

"Why don't you pick on someone your own species?"

"That, girls, is my kind of . . . Xander?!"

"Three times a fish guy."

"What, you got a shiny new car and now you're someone new?"

Faith: **Hold me.**
Xander: **Did I mention I'm having a strange night?**

"Didn't you?"

He shook his head, clearly confused by the turn she had taken. "What? No, I snuck in yesterday and peed in the pool."

"Oh." Her shoulders fell in disappointment. Then, realizing what he had done, she made a face. *"Eew."*

Coach Marin and Principal Snyder entered the building, walked through the crowded school hallways. Coach Marin, as usual, wore his school colors like a badge of honor. The principal was dressed in another gray vested suit, although the shirt and tie were different patterns than the day before.

"This is such a blow," the coach complained. "Sooner or later the rest of my boys are gonna find out. How can I ask them to swim?"

"It's a terrible, terrible tragedy," Principal Snyder said. They turned into the student lounge. "We all feel your pain, Coach. I don't know two finer boys than Cameron and . . . that other one." He stopped the coach, pointing with one finger to emphasize his point. "But I know they'd want their friends to go on and win that state championship. It's time to think about the team."

"Well, I don't have a full team as it is," Coach Marin said. "If we don't find someone by this afternoon's tryouts, we won't be eligible to compete."

"You'll find someone," Mr. Snyder assured him. "All he has to do is wear a bathing suit, right?"

The two men continued through the lounge, out of earshot. But Xander, sitting at a nearby table, had heard enough.

Gage leaned over the pool table, into his shot. He wore his team jacket, good old burgundy and gold, over a white sweater. Music from the PA almost drowned out the sharp report of the stick hitting the cue ball, the crack as the cue rolled into its target.

He was playing alone.

Sitting at the pastry bar, Buffy was also alone. Her hair was pulled into a bun, secured by a chopstick. She wore all black now, the better to blend into the shadows of the Bronze.

But it wasn't working.

Gage felt her gaze on him, looked up. She glanced away, left the bar, casually strolled to a spot behind one of the I-beams that supported the roof.

But she wasn't entirely hidden behind the beam, and he spotted her there, too. He tossed his stick onto the table, left the game.

She started to move, coming around the beam to keep him in sight.

And walked right into him.

She tried to go around the other side of the beam, but he met her there as well.

"This 'me and my shadow' act?" Gage said. "It's getting old. What do you want from me?"

Caught off guard, she tried to think on her feet. "Well, um . . . It's a little embarrassing, but see . . . I'm a swim groupie."

"Uh-huh," Gage said. Not buying it.

Buffy dug herself in deeper. "Oh yeah. There's just something about the smell of chlorine on a guy." She reached for sexy. "Oh baby."

He said "Mmm," and turned on his heel.

She chased after him, got in front of him, and brought him to a stop. "Okay, okay," she said. "Okay, obviously my sex appeal is on the fritz today, so I'll just give it to you straight. There's something lurking around making fillets out of the populace and I think you might be next."

He was no more convinced by this story than he was by the last. "Uh-huh. And you think that because—"

"Well, it's already attacked . . . it's already killed some people."

"You're one twisted sister, you know that? Cam told me about your games. Go find someone else to harass." He pushed past her and went out the door. She had blown it, big time, and couldn't even bring herself to follow him.

Even outside, he couldn't shake the creepy feeling Buffy gave him. Gage shook his head, trying to clear it. "What a psycho," he said.

He had been talking to himself, but now he noticed someone else in the alley, a tall guy in a dark coat. Handsome, but pale. The guy must have heard, because he spoke.

"Gotta be talking about Buffy," he said.

"How'd you know?" Gage asked.

"She and I . . . had this thing once," the stranger explained. "Biggest mistake of my life."

No kidding. "My condolences, dude," Gage said.

"She's a real head tripper," the guy went on. Gage was starting to be a little freaked out by the personal way this guy was talking to him. After all, they'd just met. Actually, they *hadn't* met.

"Tell me about it. Girl thinks she's God's gift or something."

"Who is she, the Chosen One?" the stranger asked.

"Exactly."

"You know," the guy continued. "What she really needs is for someone to knock her down a few notches."

"That'd be sweet," Gage said, liking the concept. "Anyone in mind?"

"You're in luck, my friend . . ."

Gage turned back to see why he was in luck, but the guy wasn't where he had been. He could still hear the stranger's voice, though, continuing.

"Just so happens . . ."

And then the guy was in front of him, even though it didn't seem like anyone could move that fast. And he was different now. His forehead was . . . thicker, somehow. And ridged. It made his eyes look smaller, beady. And his teeth were . . . well, fangs was the only word that came to mind.

"I'm recruiting."

Gage tried to scream as the guy lunged at him, growling like an animal. Gage managed to get out a couple of hoarse shouts, put his arms up. But the guy battered away his defenses. He's strong, Gage thought. Then the guy moved in, gripping Gage in an unshakable grasp, and then Gage felt the stranger's teeth bite into his neck. *They are fangs,* he thought, as they sank deep in his flesh. "Hey, get off!" he shouted. "Help! Get off of me! Help!"

But he also realized that the strength of his shouts was diminishing with every passing moment. If no one had heard yet, no one was likely to now.

Buffy left the Bronze, feeling very much defeated. She couldn't exactly watchdog Gage if he didn't want to be watchdogged. But he was next up on the feeding frenzy list, she was sure. She didn't want the skins of any more students left lying around, emptied out like old grocery bags. Especially when she knew who the next victim would be.

She heard a strangled cry, maybe because she was listening for trouble, or maybe just because she was the Slayer, and that was the kind of thing she did.

It sounded like Gage. And it sounded like he was saying something like, "Help! Get off of me! Help!"

She ran, around the corner and down the alley.

And there he was, sprawled out on the ground. Standing above him, someone dressed in dark clothes was spitting like he'd just tasted something truly *ick*-inducing.

She spun and lashed out with a kick, knocking him back away from Gage. He responded with a familiar growl. Vampire. She yanked the chopstick—sharpened to a point—from her bun. Her hair fell down around her face.

And she recognized Angel, finally, at the same moment that he recognized her.

She held the chopstick at the ready.

"Why, Miss Summers," Angel said with a cold smile. "You're beautiful."

Before she could figure out how to respond to that, he reached down, lifting Gage as easily as one would a child. Angel threw the limp swimmer at her, and they both went down in a tangle of limbs. By the time she had regained her feet, Angel was running away into the night. She didn't bother to give chase.

"Oh," Gage said, getting to his feet. He was bleeding from the bite, but otherwise okay. "Was that the thing that killed Cameron?"

"No," Buffy assured him. "That was something else."

"Something else?" he asked, surprised.

"Yeah, unfortunately we have a lot of something elses in this town," she said flatly. "G'night."

But she hadn't gone more than two steps when Gage called out. "Hey! Walk me home?"

They walked.

* * *

Sunnydale High's Olympic-sized pool was indoors, surrounded by wooden bleachers. In years past, those bleachers were seldom used, even during the swim team's meets. But this year, with the state championship within grasp, they were jammed for meets, and even practice sessions drew spectators.

The spectators today included Buffy, Willow, and Cordelia, although they had a different agenda than most of the crowd.

The team members stood at the edge of the pool, loose and relaxed. They all wore swim caps and goggles. Coach Marin shouted, "Swimmers! Take position!" and the swimmers dropped into their starting crouches, ready to dive.

He blew a short, sharp blast from his whistle. Suddenly the air was full of swimmers in motion. They hit the water, each in his own lane, and started reaching out, cupping the water in their hands, propelling themselves the length of the pool.

Coach Marin walked alongside as they went, shouting out words of encouragement. "Keep it going, keep it going," he said. "All the way to the end. All the way to the end." He repeated himself as if they were small children, or maybe big ones who were not all that bright. But then again, Buffy reflected, she had spent quite a bit of time with Cameron Walker, who she knew for a fact was no Einstein. *So maybe a little repetition is a good thing.*

"Breathe deep," the coach said. *Confirmation of theory.*

Gage stopped swimming in the middle of the pool, scanned the audience. When he saw Buffy, he waved. She gave him a little hand waggle in return.

But the coach spotted him too. "Gage, you with us or not?" he demanded. "C'mon, let's go!"

Coincidentally, Buffy had been telling Will and

Cordy, between the handfuls of popcorn that were today's lunch, about the events outside the Bronze the night before.

"He just spit it out?" Cordelia asked. "I thought Angel liked blood."

"He used to," Buffy agreed.

"Maybe his eyes were too big for his stomach?" Willow said.

"Or maybe there was something in Gage's blood Angel didn't like," Buffy offered. "Say, for example, steroids."

"That would explain all their behavioral changes," Willow said.

"And the winning streak," Cordelia added.

Willow took the logical next step. "So maybe whatever is in their blood is what's attracting this creature to them!"

"Any luck researching our fish monster?" Buffy asked Cordy.

"Zippo. We couldn't find any sea demons that match the description that Xander gave us. Not that Chicken Little's much of a witness, but—" Cordelia stopped in midsentence, distracted by something down at the end of the pool.

"Oh," Cordelia said, eyes widening. "Oh. Oh, my. That, girls, is my kind of . . ."

Buffy turned to see what the girl was looking at. A swimmer walked toward the pool, strong, muscular legs leading to a tiny, tight Speedo. Above it, a narrow waist flared to a strong chest, broad shoulders, powerful arms.

Goggles hung at his neck.

Above that, Xander's face.

"Xander?" Willow said, astonishment ringing in her tone.

"Xander?" Cordy echoed. Hearing his name seemed

to remind Xander of what he was wearing. Or, not wearing. He scrambled for a kickboard, held it in front of the little swimsuit. Behind him, for what good it did, he held his yellow swim cap.

The girls climbed down from the bleachers.

"What the hell are you doing here?" Cordelia asked him.

Xander whispered his reply. "I'm under cover."

"You're not under much," Buffy observed, stifling a giggle.

"Get out of here before someone sees you impersonating a swim team member," Cordelia instructed him.

"I don't do impersonations," Xander protested. "I tried out for the team last night. I made it."

"Really?"

"Yeah," he explained. "I figure I can keep an eye on Gage and the others when Buffy can't."

"When you're nude?" Willow asked. Buffy gave Willow a smack, and she corrected herself. "I meant to say 'changing.' "

A tweet from the coach's whistle cut the air.

"Harris," Coach Marin called. "You can flirt on your own time."

"Okie-dokie coachie," Xander said. He backed away from the girls, tossed the kickboard back toward the pile it came from, and joined the rest of the team.

Cordelia seemed almost in awe, but Buffy couldn't tell whether it was of him or of herself. "I'm dating a swimmer from the Sunnydale swim team," the cheerleader said, almost dreamily.

"You can die happy," Buffy told her.

Cordy didn't seem to hear. She was too busy watching Xander adjust his goggles as he stood with his toes at the pool's end, preparing to dive in.

"What about Jonathon?" Buffy asked Willow, trying to get back to the earlier discussion. "He involved?"

"Oh, no," Willow answered. "He just, uh . . . he sort of peed in the pool."

"Oh," Buffy said.

Xander dove.

Buffy realized what he was diving into. "Oh," she said again. This time, though, her tone was much more distressed.

Xander didn't have a lot of experience with steam rooms. For that matter, sitting around any kind of room with a bunch of guys wearing nothing but towels was pretty new to him. The fact that no one was talking made it that much worse. A long silence could be uncomfortable. A long, naked silence was downright unbearable.

So he filled the space. "Don't you guys get claustrophobic in here?" he asked. "I mean, what's the deal? You perspire a lot, you can't breathe. Or read. I mean, you could, but the pages would probably get all wet . . ."

In the locker room, just outside the steam room, there was a drain leading into the sewer system that ran beneath the school. Over the drain was a grate, a couple of feet square. Normally, the grate just sat there in the floor, as grates tend to do.

But this was not "normally." And also not normal were the clawed, scaly fingers that hooked through the grate, lifting it out of the way . . .

Buffy paced. She pretended to read a No Smoking notice on the corridor wall. Then she got so bored she actually did read it. Then she paced again. Finally, she leaned against the wall.

More finally than that, Xander came out of the locker room, a white towel draped over his head. *If he's going for the Lawrence of Arabia look,* she thought, *he hasn't quite grasped the concept.*

"You gotta love this undercover deal," he said. "Twenty minutes in a hot room with a bunch of sweaty guys."

"Where's Gage?" she asked, getting right to business.

"I don't know. He was right behind me, putting his sneakers on. But they're not the Velcro kind, so give him a couple of extra minutes." Xander tapped her on the arm as he walked off. "Tag, you're it."

Back to waiting.

Inside the locker room, Gage was indeed tying his shoelaces. As he finished, he noticed a putrid odor coming from somewhere. He sniffed. Not his shoes. He raised his arms, checking himself. Nope. He was shower-fresh.

He left the bench, walking through the deserted locker room. It smelled like a walrus had curled up inside one of the lockers and died.

The disgusting odor was even more pronounced at one particular bank of lockers. He sniffed, followed the stink to a specific locker. He opened it.

Buffy was beyond bored, and growing edgy. How long could it take for one swimmer to tie a pair of shoes? *Maybe the chlorine does something to the mental processes,* she thought. *Or the steroids. Fast in the water, slow on land.*

She was on her millionth pace when she heard him scream.

"Oh, God!" Gage called.

She shoved through the swinging doors and ran into the locker room. He was still screaming, panic in his voice. "Help! Help me! Help me!"

When she came around the bank of lockers, there he was. And there, also, was one of the fish monsters Xander had seen, closing in on him.

Buffy shoved Gage back out of the way. He hit the lockers and slid to the floor, terrified. He looked like he was in pain, but Buffy's first concern had to be the huge, slimy creature from the depths. She faced it, ready for it to make its move.

But Gage let out another scream. Something was very wrong with him. The monster wasn't attacking, so she took a calculated risk, and left it alone. *If it wants to tangle, it knows where to find me.*

Gage was curled into almost a fetal position on the floor, his back against the lockers. When Buffy approached, he reached out for her. He seemed to be in big-time agony.

"Gage?" she asked, concerned.

He screamed again, convulsing. His shirt was open, and he clutched his chest. *Food poisoning?* Buffy wondered. *Heart attack?*

Or something worse. His whole chest seemed to be heaving, skin rippling. He dug his fingers into his own flesh. Then, grabbing his skin in both hands, he pulled it apart. She'd seen that done on doctor shows, but those people had things like internal organs and rib cages beneath the flesh. Not Gage.

Still moaning, he held his own hand up and looked at it. But the skin of his hand fell off, like a discarded glove, as something wet and slick pushed up through it. The same stuff forced itself through the hole in his chest.

Buffy realized what was happening just before it rose

to its full height. One of the fish monsters was erupting from inside Gage. It sloughed off his skin like a shedding snake. Everything that had been Gage was now an empty sack on the locker room floor, and a huge, and apparently unfriendly—gill monster was looking at Buffy.

And, like most new monsters, it was hungry.

It lunged for her.

She backed up a step. And felt—or rather, smelled—the rank breath of the other one right behind her. *Whoops!*

She was surrounded by sea life. *My kingdom,* she thought, *for a fishhook.*

Chapter 9

Both creatures growled. This was not a simple fish-family reunion, then. Their intentions seemed hostile at the very least.

Buffy didn't waste any time. She gave one a quick kick, and it reeled back. Continuing her spin she lashed out with the same foot, catching the other beast in the chest. Its legs flew out from under it and it hit the floor. She snatched up a metal garbage can, hurled it at the first one. It swatted the can away as she would a fly.

She needed a weapon of some kind.

There was a lacrosse stick in a corner. She had never really understood lacrosse, but she understood a long solid object with two ends that could be used to jab and strike. She grabbed the stick, swung it into the head of one of the creatures. It roared in pain, fell away. She swung again, driving it home on the other's skull. Then, spinning around, she took a couple of swings worthy of

Mark McGwire into the ribs of the first one she'd hit. *It's feeling the pain,* she thought.

This just might work.

Which was when the other monster caught her from behind, buried its long teeth into her arm, lifted her in the air, and slammed her into a bank of lockers.

Buffy was dazed, just aware enough to know that they were about to finish her off.

But they didn't, because then Coach Marin was there, helping her up and dragging her away to safety.

And, as if scared of a fair fight, the two creatures hit the floor, sliding toward the still-open grate. They dove head-first down the drain, and were gone.

The last time she'd been in Nurse Greenleigh's office, it was to be reprimanded. This time it was to be bandaged. She sat in the same place as Cameron had, a few days earlier. Nurse Greenleigh, dressed in her white nurse clothes, looked like she had never moved away from this spot.

"I don't think that this'll need stitches," the nurse said. "But you might want to have your family physician take a look at it."

"How are you?" Giles asked her.

"I'm definitely feeling the burn."

Coach Marin flanked Giles. The librarian turned to him. "Well, the good news is, it would appear none of your team actually died."

"But the bad news is, they're monsters," Buffy added.

The coach seemed genuinely upset. "How could this happen?"

"Are you saying you don't know?" Giles asked.

"Well, you work so hard, you start winning suddenly . . . you think it's just you, you're inspiring the boys to greatness. But in the back of your mind, you start to wonder."

Giles didn't seem convinced. "You never asked the boys if they were taking anything?"

"Maybe I was afraid to," the coach admitted.

After school, Xander, Buffy, and Willow met in Willow's computer classroom. Willow sat in front of one of the machines, *which is fitting,* Xander thought, *because she actually knows how to use them.* He and Buffy were feeling their way toward the twentieth century while Will had already jumped into the twenty-first.

"There," Buffy said, pointing to something on the monitor.

Willow read. " 'Dodd McAlvy . . . torn tendon. Gage Petronzi . . . fractured wrist . . . depression . . . headaches—' "

"It's all here in the school medical records," Buffy pointed out.

"All symptomatic of steroid abuse," Willow agreed.

Xander felt like he was still a step behind. "But is steroid abuse usually linked with 'Hey, I'm a fish?' "

"There must be something else in the mix," Willow said. "But the point is, the boys were obviously drugged."

Buffy added, "And Nurse Greenleigh treated each and every one of them. She must have known."

"If steroids are that dangerous," Willow asked, "why would they do that to themselves?"

So naive, sometimes, Buffy thought. "They needed to win," she explained. "Winning equals trophies, which equals prestige for the school. You see how they're treated. It's been like that forever."

Xander jumped in. "Sure, the discus throwers got the best seats at all the crucifixions."

"Meanwhile," Buffy said, "I'm breaking my nails battling the forces of evil and my French teacher can't even remember my name."

Which Xander could actually see an upside to, around report card time. But he kept that to himself. "So what's the drill?" he asked. "Get Nurse Greenleigh?"

"Let's throw the book at her!" Willow said, maybe a little too enthusiastically.

"She probably went home for the day," Buffy said. "I think it can wait. Xander, why don't you see if you can find out what these boys are taking, or at least how they're taking it. Powder, pills, syringes—"

"I'm looking-around guy."

"What about you?" Will asked.

"Giles is loading up the tranquilizer gun," Buffy replied. "We're going fishing."

The ground beneath Sunnydale was honeycombed with sewer pipes tall enough for a person to walk through, but nasty enough that only the very wiggiest person would want to.

Buffy supposed that the same could be said of any city. *But when it's Sunnydale,* she thought, *everything's a little creepier, and ditto for the sewers.* She was glad she had her Watcher with her. And more glad that, while she was armed with only a flashlight, Giles was carrying a big old gun. He was loaded for bear, as the saying went.

Only in this case, more like loaded for barracuda.

They both saw it at the same moment, a motion just beyond the beam of her light. She raised it, shining it at the movement. Giles brought the gun up, cocked it, sighting along its length.

But she touched his arm. Only a big rat. Ooky, but

hardly supernatural. It belonged here; they were the tourists. They kept looking.

And as they turned a corner, moving deeper into the dripping, malodorous dark, neither noticed a shadowy form watching from the far end of the tunnel. Watching, and waiting . . .

Back in the steam. Xander was getting used to the nearly naked bodies of his teammates, and the small degree of modesty that paper-thin white gym towels provided.

The lack of conversation still bugged him, though. That, and the fact that, without conversation, information was hard to come by. So he did his monologue thing again, hoping to elicit a response from someone.

"I feel good," he said. "Loving this swimming. Had some carrot juice this morning, a little wheat germ mixed in . . . woke me right up. Nothing like it, huh? Breakfast of state champions, you betcha." He pumped his fist for emphasis.

He might as well have been in a room full of corpses.

Except, come to think of it, he'd already done that, and they were much more lively.

Subtlety isn't going to work with this crowd, he thought. *Time to be more direct.*

"Okay, so, when do we get our next dose?"

And, bingo. Pay dirt.

Sean, sitting catercorner from Xander, spoke up.

"What do you mean?"

"Who's carrying?" Xander elaborated. "I need a little something to improve my performance. Give me an edge. Rrrr," he growled.

Sean looked away.

Xander decided he'd been right about the subtle approach. These guys needed to be hit over the head. "The steroids? Where are they?"

This time, Sean laughed. "You're soakin' in it, bud."

"Huh?" Xander asked, not quite following.

Sean took a deep breath, blew it out. "Aromatherapy," he explained. "It's in the steam."

Coach Marin walked briskly around the pool, moving like a man with a mission. Behind him, Nurse Greenleigh rushed to keep up. "This has got to stop, Carl," she said. "Those poor children."

He glanced back at her. "What, are you a quitter? There's no room for quitters on this team."

"Do you even understand what's happening? Listen to yourself!"

"We're very close to perfecting this. We just need to adjust the mix." He reached a staircase and headed down.

Nurse Greenleigh kept right on his heels. "Carl, you can't be thinking of continuing to expose these boys."

"They're gonna be the best," the coach insisted. "I don't accept anything less." At the bottom of the stairs, he turned into a pump room that ran beneath the pool. Inside was a short staircase, and he climbed its three steps to a platform.

"They're gonna be monsters!" the nurse argued. "Carl, please. Don't make it any worse. You've already lost three."

She was still right behind him. He stopped suddenly, and turned to her. "Lost? They're not lost." He grabbed her by her upper arms, gave a mighty push, and shoved her to where there should have been a grate in the floor.

But the grate was moved to one side, and the hole was open.

With a shriek, she fell through.

And splashed into a dank, filthy grotto, about one flight down. The cold smelly water came to her waist.

"Carl! What are you doing?" she demanded, tears in her eyes.

The sewers!

He smiled down from above. "I'm just looking after my boys. They may be out of the game right now, but they're still a team," he said. "And a team's gotta eat."

"Carl!" she called again.

But he simply pushed the grate back into place. "You quitter," he said. Then he disappeared, and she heard his footsteps receding.

She backed through the water. *There has to be a way out of here,* she thought. *The water must come from somewhere.* She'd find her way out. She was no pushover. And when she got out, she'd make Carl Marin pay—

Which was when she felt clawed hands around her ankles. She was only able to let out a short shriek before she was yanked under the water.

Within a few moments, the surface was placid once more.

CHAPTER 10

Xander paced the library floor, nervous. He wasn't ordinarily a nail-bitin' guy, but this was not an ordinary situation, and he worried them to the quick as he walked.

"They're absorbing the steroid mixture through the steam," Giles said, as if he was telling anyone something they didn't already know.

"Not they," Xander said. "We. *Me.* We need to find an antidote, don't you think? The clock is ticking, people."

Willow was in a chair nearby, looking appropriately worried. Buffy sat Indian style on a table. Cordelia looked gorgeous on the steps—not especially useful, as she wasn't mixing chemicals or anything. *But cute, just the same.*

"I wouldn't break out the tartar sauce just yet," Buffy said. "It's not like you were exposed more than once."

Xander looked at her, willing her to accept reality.

"Twice?" she asked.

"Three times a fishguy."

"Oh—whoa," Willow said.

"What am I gonna do?" Xander asked, making every attempt to avoid actual whining.

"You, you, you . . . What about me?" Cordelia said. "It's one thing to be dating the lame, unpopular guy. It's another thing to date the Creature from the Blue Lagoon."

" 'Black' Lagoon," Xander corrected. His anxiety was apparent in his tone, which even he realized was verging on snappish. "The creature from the Blue Lagoon was Brooke Shields. And thank you so much for your support." He sank onto the stair below hers, head in his hands.

He was doomed.

"I think we'd better find the rest of the swim team," Buffy suggested, "and lock them up before they get in touch with their inner halibut."

"Yes, good," Giles said. "We also need to know exactly what was in this steroid gas so the hospital's toxicology lab can develop an antidote."

My new favorite word, Xander thought. *"Antidote."* It was like music.

"Well, I'll talk to Nurse Greenleigh," Willow offered, rising from her chair.

"You're really getting into this interrogation thing," Buffy said.

Willow smiled. "The trick is not to leave any marks." She headed out to find the nurse.

"On that note," Buffy said, "I think I'm gonna go have a little talk with that coach. Somehow I doubt that all he's been giving these boys is inspiration."

Xander watched her go. Giles's talk of an antidote aside, he remained convinced.

Any minute now, he thought, *I'll be breathing through gills.*

The pump room was an unpleasant place to visit. It was crowded and close and smelled like grease and sweat. Not as bad as the sewers, but still not Buffy's idea of an ideal spot to pass the time.

Which made it perfect for talking to Coach Marin, because he was not her ideal person to pass time with.

"You've got quite an imagination, missy," he said, leading her up a short flight of stairs.

He was right about that. "Right now I'm imagining you in jail," Buffy said. "You're wearing a big orange suit and—oh, look! The guards are beating you up!"

"You don't have any proof that—"

She cut him off. "Tell me what's in the steam," she insisted. *He knows—he has to.* She had no doubt of that anymore.

And, amazingly, he told her. "After the fall of the Soviet Union, documents came into light detailing experiments with fish DNA on their Olympic swimmers. Tarpon, mako shark . . . But they couldn't crack it."

"And you did. Sort of." Buffy was astonished that the swim coach, not a gentleman known for overexercising his brain cells, could succeed where who knew how many Soviet scientists had failed. *Chalk one up for American ingenuity.* But one question remained. "Why?"

"What kind of a question is that?" he asked. He seemed to genuinely not get it. "For the win. To make my team the best they could be. Do you understand we have a shot at the state championship?"

"Do you understand that I don't care? It's over. There's not gonna be any swim team." *What does it take to get through to some people?* she wondered.

And still he couldn't buy a clue. "Boy, when they were handing out school spirit you didn't even stand in line, did you?"

"No, I was in the line for 'shred of sanity.' "

As Buffy spoke, Coach Marin turned away from her, toward a cabinet of some kind, reached into a drawer. When he turned back, his hand was full of black metal. A gun.

From her vantage point it looked like a big one. Mostly hole. From which a big bullet could come blasting out at any time.

She finished her thought anyway. The "sanity" line. Not *even* a shred here. "Which you obviously skipped."

"Get in the hole," the coach demanded. He gestured with the gun toward a big square hole in the floor. The grate that should have covered it was off to the side.

She didn't move. He wouldn't really shoot her, would he?

But then again, she thought, *he's been busy turning his swimmers into gilled creatures who hide out in sewers. Not the kind of guy you want to underestimate when he's holding a gun on you.*

"In," he commanded. When she still didn't go, he barked, *"Now!"*

She sat down on the edge of the hole, legs dangling into the cool darkness below. "This isn't over."

"In!" he repeated.

She pushed off and dropped.

The water was nasty and cold, but not deep. She submerged when she hit, but surfaced again quickly. Wiping her eyes, she looked up at the coach's smiling, insane face through the hole. He waved the gun at her.

"You think I don't care about my boys," he said. "But I do. They count on me."

Something moved in the water around her, and she started. *The fish monsters?* Something else. Big and white and red, floating. It almost bumped into her as it drifted past, and it took her a moment of looking at it to realize what it was.

The corpse of Nurse Greenleigh.

Or most of it, anyway.

But there were big chunks of her missing, which was where the red came in, staining her once-white uniform.

Buffy felt herself on the edge of panic, but knew she had to keep it together. "So, what," she said. "You're just gonna feed me to them?"

"Oh, they've already had their dinner," he explained patiently, like some demented daddy. "But boys have other needs."

"No one," Cordelia said. "Willow and Giles must've rounded up the rest of the swim team."

They were at the pool, but hadn't been able to find any more of Xander's teammates. *Although,* Cordelia thought, *if Xander did a little more searching and a little less pawing at himself, we might have had more luck.*

"Does my neck look scaly to you?" he asked.

"Of course it looks scaly, the way you've been rubbing it dry like an idiot." *Don't boys know anything about skin care?* she wondered. *Moisturize, don't irritate.*

Xander stopped outside the door to the boys' locker room. "I need to look in the mirror," he said. "Wait here. But feel free to come in if you hear me scream."

He dashed inside, and she briefly considered going into the girls' locker room to check herself in the mirror there. *But no,* she thought. There was more at stake here than making sure her hair was just so and her skin wasn't in any danger as a result of Xander's paranoia. The state championship. She continued around the pool.

Anyway, he wasn't gone long. She heard a door close behind her. "Any gills yet?" she asked over her shoulder.

But instead of joining her, there was a huge splash in the pool. The tang of chlorine filled the air as the calm water was disturbed. "Xander, what are you doing?"

She looked into the water. He was swimming fast, a blur of motion and bubbles, and at first she couldn't get a good look at him.

But then his strokes became smoother, and he rushed through the water like a . . .

Well, like a fish.

"Xander?"

Because he was a fish, or a fish-man, anyway, all gills and spikes and fins and scales, and he was kind of a dark green, and this just wouldn't do at all.

Oh no!

"Oh, my God," she said. "Xander . . . it's me. *Cordelia.* I—I know you can't answer me, but God . . . this is all my fault. You joined the swim team to impress me. You were so courageous and you looked really hot in those Speedos."

What a waste! I could just cry!

He went on swimming, and there was no way to tell if he could hear her. But she felt she had to say it anyway. "And I want you to know that I still care for you, no matter what you look like," she bravely went on. "And we can still date—or not. I mean, I'll understand if you want to see other fish."

She crouched by the water's edge, wanting to make sure he understood what she was saying, while still keeping her dress dry. "I'll try to make your quality of life better, whether that means little bath toys or whatever—"

"Uh . . ." someone said in her ear. She gasped. "That's not me."

Xander stood beside her, pointing at the creature in the pool. *But if this is Xander, and he's human, then who's—*

The sea beast lunged at them.

"Oh my God!" Cordelia shrieked. "Ohhh!"

They ran. Through her panic, Cordelia was pleased to note that, at least, Xander was running like a man.

Giles closed the door of the library's book cage behind the five swim team members he had herded into it. "Stay calm, chaps," he said. "Either we'll find an effective antidote, or, uh . . ." Without a follow-up, he threw the bolt, locking them in. "Stay calm."

Willow checked her list. "Everyone's accounted for, except Sean," she said.

Xander and Cordelia, hurrying into the relative safety of the library, overheard. "I think we can safely say we found Sean," Cordelia pointed out. "He was in the pool, skinless-dipping."

"Where's Buffy?" Xander asked, figuring it was about time she start slaying something, already.

"She hasn't come back yet," Willow replied.

Which, to Xander, was just a little bit more than disturbing.

Where Buffy was, was still in the disguisting water of the tunnel beneath the pump room. There were noises all around her. Water dripping from above, low growls from here and there, unidentified sloshing and splashing.

"Great," she said to herself, turning slowly to see

them. "This is just what my reputation needs. That I did it with the entire swim team."

They were closing in, she knew. She gasped at a nearby splash. The water was being stirred up, but so far she hadn't actually seen any of them. They hadn't attacked. But they were out there, and she should have been circling her wagons except that she was the only wagon she had.

In the pump room, Xander found Coach Marin, kneeling on the floor looking at something beneath him. Xander couldn't see what it was. But since Buffy had been on her way to see the coach last time she'd been seen, he knew it wasn't something nice and sunny.

"What's up, Coach?" he asked.

Coach Marin swung around, startled. "Oh, uh, Harris. How are you feeling?" He smiled, all casual, like a four year old caught in the act.

"A little dry," Xander replied. "Nothing a lemon butter sauce won't cure." He left all pretense of humor behind. "Where's Buffy?"

The coach's gaze drifted to his side, to a fifty-gallon drum that stood near him.

Or, more accurately, to the pistol laying on top of that drum.

One of the creatures broke the surface next to Buffy. She let out a cry as it dove at her. She caught its arms, turned with it, and it sailed harmlessly past her.

But it had a friend.

This one came up behind her. She tried to push it away when the first one, still underwater, grabbed her legs in its powerful grip. It yanked her under the surface.

She tasted the foul water. It stung her eyes.

She kicked and fought, struggling not to swallow any of the water as it held her down. She could feel the thing's teeth graze her leg, trying to find purchase. Mustering all the strength she could, she kicked again, jerked her leg free.

She broke the surface, grabbed the monster.

Hurled him against the wall.

Another lunged for her. She caught its outstretched arms. The water made judo harder, but she pivoted, brought it over her shoulder. Slammed him into another wall.

Above Buffy, Coach Marin went for the gun. Xander saw him make the move, and grabbed the coach's right arm with both hands. The coach was strong, but he didn't have any leverage. Xander did. He brought Coach Marin's arm up, and drove it down again, hard, on the edge of the barrel. The coach's hand spasmed, releasing the gun.

Xander pressed the advantage, spinning and driving an elbow into Coach Marin's jaw. The older man fell back.

Buffy was getting tired. Moving through the water, fighting in it, was harder than fighting on land. It opposed her with every motion.

The fish-guys, however, thrived in it. No matter how many times she punched them or threw them or kicked them, they came back for more.

She wouldn't go down easy. But, as three of them surrounded her, edging closer with every heartbeat, she finally started to think that she might be going down.

"Buffy! Hurry! Your hand!"

It was Xander, stretching an arm down from the opening in the pump room above.

But he was as fully extended as he could get, and it was way too high to jump.

For any normal girl.

Buffy hadn't been normal for a long time. She was the Slayer.

She submerged herself, coiling herself like a spring.

And like a spring, she sprang.

Uncoiling, shooting up out of the water, just as the three gill-things came at her.

She caught Xander's wrist. He had hers.

But was he strong enough to lift her?

One of the creatures jumped up, catching her leg. Then they all started leaping, claws raking her feet, her calves. She kicked them away.

But that threatened to break Xander's grip. She tightened hers on his arm, and he began to pull her up.

The monsters weren't giving up, though. Two of them got grips on her feet. She shook them off.

"Hold on! " Xander called. "Come on!"

"Pull!" Buffy cried.

And—miraculously—he was lifting her. The monsters growled ferociously as she was raised beyond their range. She caught Xander's upper arm now, practically climbing him to get out of that hole.

Finally, she cleared the floor. Put a hand on it to help haul herself out, then her legs were free and she was on her hands and knees, choking and spitting out the wretched water.

"Ohhhh . . ." she said, trying to catch her breath. "Thanks."

"Just doing my part for our team," Xander replied, shaking a little with relief. *Not to mention, exertion. Oughta hit the weights more often,* he thought.

Buffy coughed again, shook the water out of her eyes,

and looked up just in time to see Coach Marin swinging a pipe wrench down on the back of Xander's skull.

Xander slumped to the floor, unconscious.

And Buffy kicked out, sweeping the coach's legs out from under him. The man went head-first through the hole.

She snagged his leg as he went.

"Help me!" he bellowed. "Help me!"

But Coach Marin was not a small man. He had momentum, and he had weight, and he was thrashing like a wounded buffalo.

She lost her grip.

He splashed into the water below.

Buffy flattened herself on the floor, extending her arm down. "Grab my hand!" she called to him.

He didn't even notice her there. Couldn't have made the leap that she did, anyway, she knew. But there was no other way to reach him.

"Uh, boys? Boys!" the coach said. Dark shapes closed in on him. "No, no, boys!"

And then they were on him, all of them. He disappeared in a burgundy and gold blur beneath the water, beneath the scales and fins and gills of his star swimmers.

His championship days are behind him now, Buffy realized.

Xander stirred, joining Buffy at the opening. He looked down. "Those boys really love their coach," she observed.

Some days, Xander thought, *you have to consider yourself lucky just to be walking around.* His head was still sore, and there was a tender swelling there from the pipe wrench.

But on the bright side, he still breathed through lungs instead of gills. Coach Marin had used a hand tool on him, but had not had a chance to use his gun. He hadn't been eaten or otherwise violated by any fish monsters.

And today, he was sitting in the student lounge, fully dressed and dry as a bone. His Speedo days were behind him.

To make it even better, sitting on the couch next to him was Cordelia, and across from them, Willow and Buffy. *Three lovely ladies, one guy . . . couldn't ask for a better ratio than that.*

"Let's see," he said, reviewing the rest of the day ahead. "I've got to take a make-up chem test at three, and then I'm meeting some of the guys for plasma transfusions at five. It's turned into quite the busy afternoon."

Buffy graced him with her smile. "The fun never stops with you, does it?"

"Giles seems pretty confident that the treatments are gonna work," Will said. Which was good news, as he wasn't quite sure how to tell his parents he wanted to trade in his old bed for an oversized saltwater tank.

"Turning into a Creepy Crawly wasn't in my 'Top Ten list of things to do before I turn twenty,' " he pointed out.

Cordelia turned to him. "I want you to know that you've really proven yourself to me," she said, with unexpected tenderness. "And you don't have to join the new team next year if you don't want."

For which, he thought, *my eternal gratitude. And, by the way, no kidding.*

"I'd be just as happy if you played football," she continued.

Buffy and Willow exchanged looks.

Giles entered just then, saving Xander from having to do or say something terrible to Cordelia, from which their relationship might never recover.

"The people from animal control just left," Giles said. "Our creatures have apparently made a dash for it. So to speak."

Which, Xander thought, *is about as close as Giles comes to making a funny.* Comedy, the librarian seemed to believe, was a purely Colonial invention.

"Does that mean we have to hunt them again?" Willow asked.

Buffy answered her. "No, I don't think so. I don't think we'll be seeing them anymore."

"Where do you think they'll go?" Giles asked.

Buffy looked into space for a moment, as if she were seeing something the others couldn't. "Home," she said softly.

The surf rolled in gently, waves folding upon themselves and breaking as white and frothy as a cappuccino. The beach was quiet today. Students were in school, tourists gone for the season, no surf to speak of so the surfers were elsewhere.

So there was no one on the shore to look out beyond the breaking waves. If there had been, that person might have seen a dark form break the water and take a final look back toward Sunnydale. Almost, an observer might have thought, as if saying a last goodbye.

Then, the black shape turned to the vastness of the ocean, and dove into it, striking out for the trackless distance. And if that observer had been especially sharp eyed, he or she might have seen a second shape, and a third.

All doing the same thing.

Swimming out to sea.

Going home.

Interlude

It was late—way late, Xander knew. His parents had pretty much given up worrying about when he was going to come home, so he wasn't too concerned about that. But he'd have to make it to school on time tomorrow—*today*, he corrected himself. And it'd be easier if he got some sleep rather than no sleep. Even though the night had been an eventful one, he figured at this point he could probably manage to drop off if he could get himself in the general vicinity of a bed.

He pulled the car out of the beach parking area and headed back toward town. Even though it was really cold now, unpleasantly so, he left the top down because, hey, it was a convertible, after all. And wasn't that kind of the point?

Xander figured his parents probably told themselves all kinds of stories about what it was he did with his friends at night that kept him out to all hours. It saddened him that they probably believed the typical teenage stuff. But at least they could deal with that, in their heads. If they knew what was really going on—that he'd almost become a fish-guy, for instance, or been abducted by the villainous vamp Spike, or turned into a vampire himself by a wayward wish of Cordelia's—they'd probably be a lot more worried and some therapist would be cashing their paychecks as fast as they could earn them.

So he kept them in the dark, and let them believe whatever they wanted.

Another sign of maturity, he figured, was taking into account the feelings of others. Especially when those others raised you and kept a roof over your head.

And Xander hoped that all the changes he'd gone through were at least somewhere near the road to maturity, if not right smack on it. There came a point when you got tired of the whole high school, adolescence, postpuberty, your-voice-and-body-have-changed-but-everybody-still-thinks-you're-a-useless-kid deal.

Of course, not all the changes since the Day of the Fish had been his.

Slayer Buffy had been through some of her own. She'd had to send Angel to Hell, for starters. Which, admittedly, from Sunnydale wasn't that far a trip. But she'd done it right as Willow had completed a spell Miss Calendar had left behind on a computer disk that would restore his soul to him—which made it an act of supremely bad timing with which Buffy had a hard time coping.

She'd left town, changed her name, and worked as a waitress instead of a Slayer. Personally, Xander couldn't see it. He'd watched waitresses put up with some pretty obnoxious diners. But those waitresses wouldn't have been able to decapitate said diners with a single kick. And, as much as he cared for Buffy, Xander was the first to admit that patience wasn't always her strong suit.

She had eventually made her way back to Sunnydale, though, and the Slayerettes had reassembled around her. They'd even been joined by Faith, yet another Slayer who was activated when Spike's friend Drusilla killed Kendra. Apparently there was a bug in this whole Slayer system that couldn't accommodate the fact that, while Buffy had indeed died, she hadn't stayed dead for all that long.

Faith, as far as Xander was concerned—well, especially now, but even before—had fit into the Scooby Gang better than Kendra had anyway. She more or less adopted Giles as her Watcher, and Buffy got to have a peer she could bond with—pretty unusual, considering that the whole point of the Slayer mythology was that there could be only one.

Just to complicate things further for her, Angel had returned to Sunnydale. Again, the return ticket from Hell was not so hard to get, it seemed. It'd been hard for Buffy to trust him again—harder still for the rest of them—but it seemed that Miss Calendar's spell had worked, and he was the cool and way too-good-looking, if somewhat drawn to dark, Slayer-attracting clothes, Angel.

Xander made one more circuit of downtown, making sure the town really was quiet for the night. One final patrol in the Batmobile. All the citizens appeared to be snug in their beds.

Driving past Uncle Bob's Magic Cabinet, where he had last seen Willow, reminded him of her new hobby. The whole soul restoration spell-casting thing intrigued Willow to the point that she took up witchcraft, and, despite the occasional oops, was turning out to be not half bad at it.

After most of a lifetime of knowing Willow—since they were five, anyway—their friendship had finally expanded to include the aspect of lust. Which was awkward, as Xander was still dating Cordelia and Willow was seeing Oz. They tried to keep themselves apart, even going so far as to work on a spell that would kill the attraction, but still, Oz and Cordy happened upon them in mid-kiss, and it was an unpleasant scene.

Like it was our fault or something, Xander thought. Imprisoned by Spike in the Factory, they both believed they were going to die. *We never would have kissed if we thought we were going to have to live with it. Who knew that Oz would be able to smell Willow and find them there? Who knew he'd have Cordelia with him when he did?*

Cordy just couldn't see the kissing part—*okay, some might call it making out*—as the response to a life-threatening situation that it so clearly was. She thought there was more to it than that. Sometimes, it just didn't pay to be rescued.

The upshot of it was unpleasant, primarily, because for a while there, Xander had had the option of quieting Cordelia by planting his lips on hers. Without that freedom, her sharp mouth returned to its old habits, which included—high on the list of habits, in fact—making those around her miserable with her sarcastic and insulting comments, and passing judgment on those who didn't live up to her own standards.

Which, by her definition, was—well, everybody.

Oz, not surprisingly, turned out to be a little more understanding than Queen Cordy. He and Willow had—eventually—renewed their relationship, leaving Xander a swinging single again. *Only,* he observed, *without so much of the swinging.*

As landmarks of personal growth went, Xander figured turning eighteen was one of the biggies. That life event, it seemed, was a little more troublesome for Slayers than for the general populace—as if the whole bit about not getting to have a real life because you spent practically every night fighting evil and badness and such wasn't bad enough. On the bright side, not that many Slayers lived to be eighteen, so it was seldom a problem.

But Buffy did. And the Watchers' Council had this rule that when a Slayer hit that mark—passing her prime Slayer years, Xander guessed—they put her through a test they called the Cruciamentum.

Nice name for a birthday party.

What it meant was that she had to face down a particularly bad vamp, without her powers. She could use whatever skills she had learned over the years, but she had no extra strength, lightning reflexes—all the stuff that being a Slayer had given her, was gone.

And the kicker was, the Slayer wasn't allowed to know any of this. She was somehow supposed to figure it out as she went.

The idea was that a vampire would be locked into a house, and the Slayer would be locked in with him, and only one would come out alive. But this vampire escaped the house, and took the battle to Buffy's own home, threatening her mom. At this turn of events, Giles defied the council by telling Buffy what was going on and helping her track and defeat the vampire. The council was pleased with Buffy's powerless performance, but not so much with Giles's defiance. They kicked him off the council, leaving Buffy Watcherless.

Nice guys.

Sunnydale was asleep. Xander knew that he should join them. He pulled the vehicle to the curb in front of his parents' silent home. Opened the door, climbed out, closed it as quietly as he could. The car would be here tomorrow. It wasn't like he had to get all his driving done in one night. He had a lifetime of driving ahead of him, he knew. He'd have his own car, one of these days. This was his last year of high school. He'd been through plenty of changes, but pretty soon, there would be that big one, the leap into the world of adult cares and responsibilities. Manhood. Maybe, some day, marriage-hood and fatherhood. And then he'd have a teenager, and his teenager would stay out most of the night, driving around town in borrowed wheels. And when the adult Xander saw his kid at the breakfast table the next morning, instead of giving him the fifth degree, he'd have to make sure he remembered to smile, pat his offspring on the back, and say, "Congratulations."

Xander went inside and tiptoed up to his room. In spite of the day's events, Sunnydale High was still standing, and would be waiting for him in a very few hours. He meant to be there for it.

Chapter 11

The cavern was full of smoke and snarls. Buffy couldn't tell who was where—she could hear the demons but not see them. Which meant they couldn't see her.

Which could have been a good thing, except that she wasn't alone here. She needed to worry about Giles, her Watcher—*well, former Watcher,* she reminded herself—and Willow and Xander and Faith. Though Faith, being a Slayer too, could probably take care of herself.

But the point was—*focus,* she told herself—there were demons, nasty ones, and they needed to be dealt with. She'd already taken out a couple. But even one still walking around in the fog was plenty dangerous, especially to her friends.

Through the mist, a point of light moved into the cave. Buffy could barely make out Willow, carrying a candle, chest high. Willow spoke a few words of Latin, and blew out the flame.

A sudden wind swept through the cavern, and the smoke cleared.

The demon was suddenly visible. There was just one of them left standing, Buffy saw. Her skin was a steely bluish gray. She was many-horned, with long pointed ears, and a mouthful of big unpleasant teeth. If they had beauty pageants in demonland, this one was not going to be a winner.

Probably not Miss Congeniality, either.

Buffy charged her.

She caught the demon just as she was turning around, slamming into her and knocking her to the ground. The demon's strength was enormous, and it took everything she had to hold her down while Giles joined her. She was suddenly thankful for her Slayer powers—her recent experiment at living without them hadn't turned out so well, and this ugly beast would have already ripped her head off and decorated the wall of her nest with it if she had been plain old mortal Buffy Summers.

Giles grabbed the hideous thing's arm and they lifted her to her feet, back up against the cave wall. Its strength was too much for Giles, though. She hurled him into the far wall, knocking the wind out of him.

Buffy held on, pressed the demon against the wall, and shouted to Faith.

"Now!"

Faith raised a ceremonial broadsword, and covered the distance in a few swift steps. She drove the sword into the demon's heart. The creature let out a long death scream.

When Faith withdrew the blade, it was red with blood.

Buffy let go. The demon plunged forward, dead, and landed next to Giles, who regarded the corpse with horror.

"I think that was the last," he said.

Willow came into the open center of the cavern, still clutching the extinguished candle in its elaborate holder.

"Will, are you okay?" Buffy asked.

"Yeah, I'm fine," Willow replied. "The shaking is a side effect of the fear."

Buffy helped Giles to his feet. He wasn't hurt, just a little dazed by the ferocity of the attack, she thought.

"Thank you," he said, still a tad breathless.

"Well, if it wasn't for that clouding spell—" Buffy gestured to Willow.

"Yeah," Willow said. "It went good! Nothing melted like last time."

"These babes were wicked rowdy," Faith said. "What's their deal?" All the demons they'd encountered here were clearly female, which was, in Buffy's experience, a little unusual in the demon world. *Feminism in action? Demonic suffragettes? Giles will know,* she thought.

"I wish I knew," Giles said. He turned over the last-killed, looked into a face only a plastic surgeon could love. "Most of my sources have dried up, since the council relieved me of my duties. I was aware that there was a nest here, but quite frankly, I expected it to be vampires. These are new."

"And improved," Buffy added.

"Yes, I'm sorry. I should have been better prepared, and I should never have allowed Willow and, uh . . . and, uh . . ." he trailed off.

A sheet of cardboard shifted, over against a far wall. Everyone tensed, suddenly on guard for another assault. But the cardboard continued to slide, and then Xander appeared from underneath it. He pushed himself unsteadily to his feet, breathing heavily.

"I'm good," Xander assured them "We're fine over here. Just a little bit dusty."

He climbed down from the pile of trash in which he'd been hiding. "Good show, everyone. Just great," he continued, clapping his hands together. "I think we have a hit."

"Are you okay?" Willow asked him.

"Tip top," he said, not very convincingly. "Really. If anyone sees my spine laying around, just try not to step on it."

"Xander, one of these days you're gonna get yourself hurt," Buffy said.

Faith put in her two cents. "Or killed."

"Or both," Buffy went on. "And you know, with the pain and then the death, maybe you shouldn't be leaping into the fray like that. Maybe you should be fray-adjacent."

Xander was clearly hurt by the implication. Buffy felt bad for him—but not as awful as she'd have felt if he'd been physically hurt during the fighting. "Excuse me?" he said. "Who, at the crucial moment, distracted the lead demon by allowing her to pummel him about the head?"

Faith didn't seem to share Buffy's empathy. "Yeah, that was real manly the way you shrieked and all," she said.

"I think you'll find that was more of a bellow," Xander protested.

Buffy changed the subject. "What should we do with the trio here? Should we burn them?"

Willow piped up at that.

"I brought marshmallows!" she said with a wide smile. The others looked at her in astonishment. "Occasionally," she continued, "I am callous and strange."

Giles tried to steer the conversation back on track. "I

expect we can leave them," he said. "I'm more interested in finding out what they are, and whether we can expect more of their kind."

"I hope not," Buffy said, remembering their incredible strength. "They're way too fit."

"I say, bring 'em on," Xander announced loudly.

Giles put a hand on Xander's shoulder, attempting, Buffy thought, to lead the young man back to something resembling reality. "Xander," Giles said, "I think in the future, it would be best if you hung back to the rear of the battle. For your own sake."

Xander wrinkled his forehead and spoke in a high-pitched voice. "But gee, Mr. White. If Clark and Lois get all the big stories, I'll never be a good reporter."

"Hmm?" Giles asked, clearly not getting it.

"Jimmy Olsen jokes are pretty much gonna be lost on you, huh?" Xander said.

"Sorry," Giles said.

"It's okay."

They left the cavern, leaving the three demon corpses that littered the ground, and went out into the night.

CHAPTER 12

The next day dawned crisp and clear. It was January. Less-than-super bowl games were over, but the Superbowl loomed, and football fever had swept the school. Xander, hanging out on Sunnydale High's quad, longed for the feel of the old pigskin in his hands.

Not enough to have taken up Cordelia's suggestion last year that he join the team or anything—those guys got hurt. He didn't want to spend his senior year in a cast. But there was something about this season that made him want to feel the sting of it in his hands, watch a perfect pass spiraling from his arm. *That old Y chromosome, acting up.*

And there were some guys tossing a ball around the quad. He could hear the smack of the ball against flesh as they caught it.

"Hey! Doug," he called. "Toss me one!" Xander bounced up and down, plaid shirttails flapping where they dangled out from beneath his bright red sweat-shirt.

Doug, a stocky guy in a letter jacket, was actually on the team. He shot Xander a look and then threw the ball to Les.

"Les, man!" Xander shouted. "I'm open!"

Les tossed it back to Doug.

And now there were cheerleaders watching.

This is going to get embarrassing, Xander realized, *if no one throws me the ball.*

"Buddy!" he called, unable to prevent a note of desperation from creeping into his voice. "Doug, right here, man! Right here! Doug, please!"

Doug relented, threw a high pass his way.

"All right," Xander said, running to snag the ball. "It's all me—"

But it wasn't.

The ball bounced off his fingertips, and landed in the lap of a student named Jack O'Toole. *Well,* Xander corrected himself, *not his lap, exactly.* More like, his *lunch,* knocking over a can of soda and squishing a sandwich.

And "student" wasn't even really the word to be used in reference to O'Toole, since it carried that connotation of studying, which was something Jack seemed to make every effort not to do. He was a senior, and had been so for three years that Xander knew of. Never quite pulled together the grades to move on, but didn't seem interested in doing the drop-out thing either.

Maybe he was afraid that would leave him without an acceptable number of people to terrorize.

Jack stood up from the remains of his lunch, football in hand. He was unshaven and old enough for it to make a difference, with short, light brown hair. He wore a dark brown leather jacket over a plain white V-necked T-shirt. A medallion hung from a leather thong at his neck. From the glare he was getting, Xander knew he had just written his own name at the top of Jack O'Toole's list. He tried to defuse things.

"Boy, I am so sorry. Doug's arm is kinda like spaghetti, we're all so very sad for him. Is your lunch okay?"

"What are you," Jack asked, "retarded?"

"No," Xander said, stammering a little. "I had to take that test when I was seven, a little slow in some stuff, mostly math and spatial relations, but certainly not 'challenged' or anything. Can I get you another soda?"

"I ought to cut your face open," Jack hissed. *If he's doing Clint Eastwood in* Dirty Harry, Xander thought, *he's got it down.*

"Hey, hey, whoa," Xander said. "It was an accident. Cool down."

Jack looked him over with an expression somewhere between amusement and menace. "You wanna be starting something?" he asked.

"What? Starting something? Like that Michael Jackson song, that was a lot of fun . . ." He did a little dance step as he sang. " 'Too high to get over—yeah yeah.' Remember . . . that fun song . . ."

Jack didn't seem impressed. "I get my buddies together, we're gonna kick your ass till it's a brand new shape." He pushed the ball into Xander's hands. "Now get outta here."

Xander got.

As he headed back toward the quad, Doug called to him. "Yo, man! The ball!"

Xander tossed it back to him, all interest in football gone for now. Cordelia was standing in front of him, having seen the whole exchange. *Great,* he thought. *It's always better to have your lowest moments observed by your ex.*

"Boy, of all the humiliations you've had that I've been witness to," Cordelia said, "that was the latest."

"I could've taken him," Xander insisted.

"Oh, please. O'Toole would macrame your face. He's a psycho. Which," she added, "is still a lot cooler than being a wuss."

"Why is it," Xander asked, glancing at Jack, "that I've come face-to-face with vampires, demons, the most hideous creatures Hell ever spit out, and I'm still afraid of a little bully like Jack O'Toole?"

"Because unlike all those other creatures that you've come face-to-face with," Cordelia explained, "Jack actually noticed you were there."

This was, Xander reflected, one of those times when it was easy to remember why he and Willow had formed the I Hate Cordelia Club when they were kids. "Why am I surprised by how comforting you're not?"

"It must be hard when all your friends have, like, superpowers," Cordy went on. "Slayer, werewolves, witches, vampires. And you're like this little nothing. You must feel like Jimmy Olsen."

Remarkably astute, he thought, considering the *who* that it was coming from. "I was just talking to—" he began with a chuckle. But he cut himself off. "Hey! Mind your own business."

"Ooh, I struck a nerve. The Boy That Had No Cool."

Xander couldn't have said why, after all these years, he still felt the need to defend himself against Cordy's verbal attacks. Some deep-rooted insecurity, maybe? Whatever the reason, he did, even though it was always hopeless.

"I happen to be an integral part of that group and I happen to have a lot to offer."

"Oh, please." She started to walk away from him.

"I do!"

She spun around on him. "Integral part of the group? Xander. You're the . . . the useless part of the group. You're the Zeppo."

He got that reference, unfortunately. The Marx Brother no one remembered. Gummo had better lines. Even Groucho, Harpo, and Chico forgot he existed half the time.

" 'Cool,' " Cordelia continued, throwing a look toward where Jack O'Toole still worked on what remained of his lunch. "Look it up. It's something that a subliterate that's repeated twelfth grade three times has and you don't."

She turned away again, leaving Xander to his verbal defeat. As she went, he heard her say to herself, "There was no part of that that wasn't fun."

Xander ignored the lunch on his cafeteria tray. Spaghetti with some kind of mystery meat sauce, a roll, an apple. He could smell it, but that didn't make him especially want to eat it.

He sat with Oz, who listened with infinite patience to his rant.

"But, it's just that it's buggin' me," Xander was saying. "This cool thing. I mean, what is it? How do you get it? Who doesn't have it? And who decides who doesn't have it? What is the essence of cool?"

"Not sure." Oz said. *Succinct, as usual. Guy even got to change his name to something cool,* Xander thought. *Almost no one even remembered that he was really Danny Osbourne. Oz. Succinct. And cool.*

"I mean, you yourself, Oz, are considered more or less cool. Why is that?"

"Am I?" Oz popped a potato chip into his mouth.

"Is it about the talking?" Xander asked. "You know, the way you tend to express yourself in short, noncommittal phrases?"

"Could be."

"No," Xander said, suddenly seeing the light. "You're in a band. That's like a business-class ticket to cool with complimentary mojo after takeoff. I gotta learn an instrument. Is it hard to play guitar?"

"Not the way I play it."

"Okay," Xander continued. "But on the other hand, eighth grade I'm taking flugelhorn and getting zero trim, so the instrument thing could be a mislead. But you need a *thing*. One *thing* nobody else has. What do I have?"

"An exciting new obsession," Oz replied. "Which I feel makes you very special."

Xander didn't miss the implied sarcastic quote marks. "Now with the mocking, which I can handle because I know I'm right about this. I'm on the track. Just need to find my *thing*."

"It seems like you're overthinking it," Oz offered with a shrug. "I mean, you've got some identity issues, it's not—"

"—the end of the world," Giles said.

Buffy looked at him, amazed that he had even raised the idea. He wouldn't have said it if he didn't mean it, though. The council may have fired him, but only because he was trying to save her skin when her Cruciamentum went all kerflooey. As far as she was concerned, he was still her Watcher, and she trusted him completely.

"Can they do that?" she asked.

They were in the school library, where Giles had been doing some research into the demons they'd defeated the night before. It was 5:20, school long since over, so they knew their conversation wouldn't be overheard.

"They seem fairly committed," he replied. "The Sisterhood of Jhe is an apocalypse cult; they exist solely to bring about the world's destruction. And we've not seen the last of them. More will follow."

"And they're in Sunnydale for what? Demon Expo?"

Giles took off his glasses, gave her the stern look. "Buffy, this is no laughing matter."

"Hence my no laughing."

"I'm sorry," Giles said. "I know I'm no longer your official Watcher, but—"

The library door swung open with a squeak, interrupting him.

"Hey," Oz said, by way of greeting.

"Hey," Buffy said back. Full moon tonight; she'd almost forgotten.

Oz walked past them, into the book cage.

Giles glanced at his watch. Darkness came early on these late winter days, Buffy knew. "Um," Giles said, "you're cutting it a bit close."

Oz closed the cage door behind himself, started to shake off his jacket. "Well, you know me."

Buffy went back to the topic at hand, namely, the end of the world. "Well, do we know why they're here?"

"I think so," Giles said. He reached for a book in which he'd found some bit of data or other. "Based on some artifacts I found with them, and taking into account the current astral cycle—"

She cut him off. "Giles, I don't need to see the math."

He put the book back down on his desk and said, very matter-of-factly, "They intend to open the Hellmouth."

So he wasn't exaggerating with the apocalypse talk. "The Hellmouth. The one that opens—"

"About twenty feet from where you're standing," Giles finished.

She looked at an empty spot of floor. Empty, from this angle. From below—not so much.

And in the cage, a fully transformed werewolf Oz gripped the cage's wire with clawed paws. Almost as if sensing the fear in the room, he threw his head back and howled.

"And if it opens?" Willow asked.

It was the end of school, the next day. Another cold, sunny one. They walked together on the grass in front of the school building. Around them, other kids were heading home to do homework or watch TV, going to their after school jobs, planning dates and parties.

No such luxury for the Slayer.

"Do you remember the demon that almost got out the night I died?" Buffy asked. Spoken casually—she really had largely put it behind her.

"Every nightmare I have that doesn't revolve around academic failure or public nudity is about that thing," Willow assured her. "In fact, once I dreamed that it attacked me while I was late for a test and naked."

"Well, it'll be the first to come out," Buffy said. "And Giles says it won't be the worst by a long shot. The world will be overrun with demons unless we stop it."

"Do we know when this is supposed to happen?"

"Giles is trying to narrow it down," Buffy answered. "If you're up for it, we're heading into deep research mode."

Willow sounded positively eager. "I'd be offended if you haven't already counted me in."

"Thanks, Will. There's something about this one . . . it scares me. I need my Willow."

"You don't have to be afraid—"

At which point, both girls jumped out of their skins at the manic honking of a car horn, right behind them.

They spun, adrenaline pumping.

Xander.

But, Xander in a car.

And not just any car. One of those boats from the fifties, all chrome and fins and sheer, gas-guzzling mass. A convertible, no less. Mint green. The radio blared.

Xander smiled behind his sunglasses. "You girls need a lift?"

"What is this?" Buffy asked.

"What do you mean, what is it? It's my *thing!*" Xander said.

"Your thing?" Willow repeated.

"My thing."

Buffy made a face. "Is this a penis metaphor?"

"It's my thing that makes me cool!" Xander explained. "You know, that makes me unique. I'm car guy. *Guy with a car.*"

"How can you afford it?" Willow asked him.

"Uncle Rory, stacking up the DUIs, letting me rent this bad boy till he's mobile again." Xander turned the music down.

Buffy fished for something to say about it. All she could come up with was, "Well, it's nice."

"Could you sound a little less enthused?" Xander said.

"Sorry."

"Evil," Willow offered, by way of explanation.

"Big?" Xander asked.

"Biggest," Buffy said. "Maybe more than I can handle."

Xander pulled off the shades, suddenly serious. "Then we'll handle it together," he said. "You know I'm here for you. Just tell me what I can do."

"Take two glazed, two cinnamon, couple creme-filled, and a jelly," Xander told the doughnut shop clerk. The air in the little store was cloyingly sweet. "No, no, let's round that out to four jellies."

Maybe Cordelia was right. I am the Zeppo.

The biggest evil Buffy had ever faced, and his job? Fetch doughnuts, Xander. Keep out of the way of the real soldiers, Xander.

He resented it. But not so much that he wouldn't do what he was asked. *An army fights on its stomach, or something like that. If the Slayer and her Slayerettes need doughnuts, then doughnuts there shall be.*

There was, he realized, only one thing that could make this worse.

And then she walked in the door.

"Ooh, some evil going on?" Cordelia asked. "It must be big for them to entrust you with this daredevil mission."

"Cordelia," he said in greeting. "Feel free to drop dead of a wasting disease in the next twenty seconds."

"Again I strike the nerve." She sounded quite pleased with herself. Which was, after all, her usual state of being. "I am a surgeon of mean."

He took his box of doughnuts and walked out the door. "I'm kinda busy right now, okay?"

Cordelia let him get all the way to his car, parked in front of the shop, before she stopped him. "Right, Buffy needs your help. Can you say 'expendable'?"

"You think you know everything—"

"I think I know you," she said.

"That's a laugh."

"Oh, what," Cordelia said. "You got a shiny car and now you're someone new. Like anybody cares about—"

She was interrupted by a blond girl walking up the sidewalk toward him. And what a blond. Young and beautiful and most definitely hot, with a figure-hugging sweater that showed plenty of figure. *Lucky sweater,* Xander thought.

And she was talking to him.

"Is that your car?" she asked.

He lowered his voice an octave. "Why yes, it is."

She looked at the vehicle, admiringly, and said " '57 Chevy Bel Air, 283 C.I.D, solid lifter, fuel injected v8?"

He knew she had the name right, anyway. The rest, he wasn't so sure about. It wasn't like Uncle Rory had given him a crash course or anything. "Uh . . . very possibly."

"How does she handle?"

"Like a dream," he replied, still barely believing this goddess was talking to him. "About warm, sticky things. Would you like to go for a little drive?"

"You busy?" she asked.

Right.

The day I'm too busy to spend time driving around town in a classic convertible with the prettiest girl who ever just walked up and started talking to me . . .

Well, just bury me, 'cause I'll be dead.

"Just gotta drop this stuff off, and then I'd describe myself as 'expendable.' " That last was for Cordy's benefit, and he watched her to make sure she caught it. She did.

He opened the door for the blond. She sat down, and he closed it behind her, ever the gentleman. Instead of going to his own door, he stepped off the sidewalk into the backseat, put the doughnut box down, and then climbed into the driver's seat.

It didn't go quite as smoothly as he had envisioned it.

She didn't even seem to notice.

Her name, it turned out, was Lysette.

She liked cars.

And that pretty much defined her, as far as Xander could tell.

They were at the Bronze. It was dark out. She was talking.

Still.

". . . and then, you know, I started seeing Dave Peck. Had a Thunderbird, engine completely tricked out, but the upholstery was kinda shot, so then I started seeing his friend Mike, not the Mike with the Mercedes, the Mike with the Mustang, an '82, v6, you know the look . . ."

His only salvation was remembering the expression on Cordy's face when he'd driven off with Lysette. That, at least, was worth some amount of torture.

Maybe not this much.

But she is such the babe.

Even so, when he spotted Angel coming into the crowded club, it was like seeing salvation.

"Angel!" Xander called, practically leaping off his stool. He waved the vampire over. "Buddy. Friend buddy. You want to sit and talk?"

"I'm looking for Buffy," Angel said, in his usual brusque manner.

You'd think a guy would learn some etiquette in almost two hundred and fifty years, Xander thought.

"Library, last I saw."

"Something's happening," Angel told him. "I've seen portents—"

No news there. "The apocalypse. They're on top of it."

"I don't think they know what they're dealing with." Angel sounded genuinely concerned.

"Let's go there!" Xander suggested, feeling the lifeline slipping from his grasp. "And tell them that."

"No," Angel said. "It's best you stay out of harm's way."

"But I could help . . ." Xander said, but Angel was already at the door. The lifeline was gone.

As if to confirm that, Lysette asked, "Hey, you wanna go for another drive?"

He walked her to the car, parallel-parked at the curb close to the Bronze's front door. "You know, it's not like I haven't helped before," he explained. He'd finally turned the conversation away from cars and toward himself. *Although, I'm not entirely sure she's listening anymore. But, oh well . . . it's not like I was listening to her.* "I've done quality violence for those people, do they even think about that?"

His pretense at chivalry gone, he simply opened the driver's side door. She got in, scooted over. He stepped in behind her, slamming the door.

He cranked the ignition, threw the car into gear, and started to pull out of the parking space.

"I mean, they act like I'm some sort of klutz—"

He hadn't gone two feet before the car stopped.

But not because of anything he had done. At least, anything intentional.

It stopped, because that's what tends to happen when one runs into another car.

Which is what he had done. There was a loud crunching of metal, and the tinkle of glass hitting the ground.

"Oh God," Xander said. "Are you all right?" A rhetorical question, since he could see that she was fine.

He got out of the car, and Lysette followed.

"Oh God," he said again. "Stay calm. Little fender bender, it's not—"

The driver's door of the car he had hit opened, and the driver emerged.

Jack O'Toole.

Homicide in his eyes.

"—the end of the world."

CHAPTER 13

Oz stood in his cage and growled.

"He's cranky," Willow said.

"It's a good night for it," Buffy agreed. They sat in the darkened library, with just enough light to read by. The table before them was piled high with books they'd gone through looking for information that might help avert the coming apocalypse.

"Can't dogs sense when there's an earthquake, and they bark?" Willow asked. "Or cows lie down or something?"

Buffy ignored her, reading out loud from the text in her lap. " 'Sisterhood of Jhe. Race of female demons fierce warriors.' Eew. 'Celebrate victory in battle by eating their foes.' They couldn't just pour Gatorade on each other?"

Giles stormed into the room, mumbling half to himself. "Council wouldn't even take my calls," he said. He sounded furious. "Idiots!" Then, to the girls, he asked, "Anything useful in the books?"

"Not wildly," Buffy replied. She closed the one she'd been reading from.

"We still have the books of Pherion to go through," Willow pointed out.

But Buffy didn't want to read more. She wanted to be doing something. Anything.

"I'm getting itchy feet, Giles," she said. "We don't turn up something soon, I'm gonna hit the streets. Maybe check out Willy's."

"Fine," Giles said. He was headed for the door himself.

"Where are you going?" Willow asked him.

Giles took his coat from a hook, began tugging it on. "Um, to try and contact the spirit guides," he said. "They exist out of time, have knowledge of the future. I have no idea if they'll respond to my efforts, but I have to try. All we know is that the fate of the entire world rests on it."

He came back to the table, looked at the open doughnut box.

"Did you eat all the jellies?" he asked.

"Did you want a jelly?" Buffy said.

He sounded hurt. "I always have a jelly. I'm always the one that says, 'Let's have jelly in the mix.' "

"We're sorry," Willow said. "Buffy had three."

Buffy gave her a look. *Ratted out by my best friend.*

"No matter," Giles suggested. "Have Xander make another run."

Buffy spoke firmly. "No. Xander's out of this. He nearly got killed last time we fought. This whole thing will be easier if we know he's safe."

* * *

"Oh. Gosh, Jack. Are you okay?" Xander asked, trying not to sound panic-stricken. He looked at the cars. His was fine, but Jack's had a broken taillight and some damage to the fender. "I am really sorry about that. Your car came out of nowhere."

"I was *parked,*" Jack said. His voice still had that sinister hush to it.

"Exactly," Xander said. "Look, I can cover the damages. I don't have insurance in the strictest sense of the word, but I have a little money . . . the important thing is that we're all all right, and we can work this out like two reasonable—"

There was the faintest *ting* as Jack whipped his knife from its scabbard. He held it up in front of him and the broad blade caught the glow from the streetlights.

It was the biggest knife Xander had ever seen outside of a pirate movie.

"—frontiersmen . . ."

"Where do you want it?" Jack asked. Like it was a foregone conclusion that Xander would take it somewhere.

"What?"

"Where do you want it?" Jack repeated.

"I'm fairly certain I don't want it at all," Xander said abruptly. "But thank you."

"Wow, cool knife," Lysette said from behind Xander. He was beginning to regret ever having given her that first ride.

"Yeah, great knife," he agreed. "Although I think it may technically be a sword."

"She's called Katie," Jack said. He moved it back and forth, letting the light play across its blade.

Her blade, Xander corrected.

"You gave it a girl's name," Xander noted. "How very

serial killer of you." To the girl, he said, "Lysette, I think we should be going."

But Jack grabbed him, turned him around, and held the knife against his face. He could feel the sharp edge on his cheek, not quite cutting. Shaving the day's whiskers, though.

"Are you scared?" Jack asked.

Xander was pretty sure what answer Jack wanted to hear. "Would that make you happy?" he asked. He caught the cracking sound of his own voice. *Affirmative,* he thought. *Scared.*

Jack moved the cold blade back and forth across Xander's cheek and neck. *Takes good care of her, too. Nice and sharp.* "Your woman looking on, you can't stand up to me? Don't you feel pathetic?"

"Mostly I feel Katie," Xander answered sincerely.

Jack pressed the blade a little harder into Xander's flesh. "You know what the difference between you and me is?"

"Again, Katie's springing to mind."

"Fear," Jack said. "Who has the least fear."

"And it has nothing to do with who has the big, sharp—"

Jack whipped the knife away from Xander's face and slapped the pommel into Xander's hand. Now Xander had the big sharp knife. Jack took a step back, motioned Xander toward him with both hands. Giving him a clear shot.

"Come on," he prompted.

Xander felt the comforting weight of the weapon in his hand. Tried to picture plunging it into Jack's bullying heart. *Just like staking a vamp,* he thought.

But he couldn't do it. Difference is, a vampire's already been dead once.

"I wanna go for a drive," Lysette whined, uninterested in this latest turn of events. "I'm bored."

"Oh, gee," Xander said, looking away from Jack for a moment. "I'm really sorry my life or death situation isn't exciting enough—"

Jack took advantage of Xander's divided attention. He grabbed Xander, slamming him backward onto the Chevy's hood. Snatching Xander's hand, he turned it, pushing the point of Katie's blade up against Xander's throat. Xander could almost taste the sharp, oiled steel.

From the outside.

Then a bright light shone in Jack's eyes. "Hey! What's going on?" a voice demanded. The thug let Xander go and backed away, Katie suddenly vanishing.

Xander straightened and saw a police officer approaching. He trained a flashlight on Jack and took in the scene.

"Nothing," Jack said. "Just rasslin'."

"O'Toole. What a surprise." The cop knew him. *Guess that figures,* Xander thought. Then, to Xander, he said, "He attack you?"

Say yes! Xander thought. *With a knife the size of Rhode Island!*

But he couldn't do it. He'd defused Jack before. He knew he could do it again. *The guy's not all bad,* he thought. *Better to stay in his good graces.* Getting Jack arrested would just aggravate him, and he wouldn't stay locked up forever.

"No," he finally said, giving the officer a big, we's-all-just-friends-here smile. "Just blowin' off steam. Two guys rasslin'. But not in a gay way," he hastened to add.

"Do it somewhere else, huh?" the cop said. He left them alone.

When Xander looked back at Jack, he realized Jack was just staring at him, grinning.

"What?"

"That was all right," Jack said. "Coulda narked on me, didn't do it. Decent of you." He paused. "I like you."

Suddenly Xander wasn't at all sure if being friends with Jack was better or worse than being enemies. "Yay?"

"You two wanna have some fun?" Jack asked.

Now Lysette was interested. "Like, with driving?"

"Yeah," Jack said.

Xander knew this had to be a bad idea. What he didn't quite know was how to get out of it. "What do you have in mind?" he stalled.

"I was on my way to get the boys," Jack said. "Gonna cruise around." He gestured toward the convertible. "We'll take your wheels."

"What about your car?" Xander asked.

Jack gave the damaged vehicle a long look. "It ain't mine."

Jack climbed into the Chevy's passenger seat. Lysette slid in beside him, in the middle. Xander sat behind the wheel. "Great," he said, without enthusiasm. "Where to?"

"Gonna get the boys!" Jack announced.

"Yeah. Great," Xander said. "Where are the boys?"

It just had to be, Xander thought, *something like this. Had to.*

They were in the cemetery. One of Sunnydale's many. Jack stood next to a grave, waving a chicken foot over it as he recited an incantation. Xander wouldn't have taken him for a student of the Black Arts, but, so much for stereotyping.

"He calls forth, the spirit of Uurthu, the restless, no

one shall speak," Jack was saying. "He shall arise! Hear me, the blood of the Earth shall restore him—"

He dropped the chicken foot, drew Katie, and sliced open his own palm. Blood from his hand dripped onto the grave.

"And he shall arise," Jack continued. "Shall arise!"

Didn't seem like much of a ritual to Xander, who had seen one or two doozies in his time. Lysette didn't seem too impressed either—bored to distraction was more like it.

But results were what counted, in the ritual business. And this one got results. Someone—presumably the "he" of which Jack had been speaking—arose.

Two fists shoved their way through the grave's hard-packed earth, followed by a crewcut-coiffed head. As he clawed his way up from the ground, Xander saw that he'd been buried, in a questionable display of taste, in a letter jacket with a big Sunnydale "S" on the chest, and a dirty T-shirt.

And that, sometime before being buried, he'd been shot in the head. There was a big, puckered bullet hole just over his left eye.

He looks like Moose, from the "Archie" comics, Xander thought. *Well, if Moose was real. And had been shot, and then buried.*

"Buddy!" the dead guy shouted.

Jack spread his arms wide, a huge smile on his face. "Bob, you big hideous corpse, come here!"

Bob threw himself into Jack's arms and gave him a big dead-guy hug.

Lysette, no longer bored, gave a blood-curdling scream and ran for her life.

"I'll call you—" Xander called after her disappearing form.

Jack and his friend were still doing the reunion thing, laughing and pounding each other on the back, the way manly guys did. Even manly zombies, it seemed.

"Man, you *raised* me!" Bob shouted. His normal speaking voice seemed to be a shout. Xander wondered if that was a side effect of having spent time in the quiet of the grave. But Bob was a big side-of-beef kind of guy—Xander figured quiet and low-key were alien concepts to him.

"I told you grandpappy could work that mojo," Jack said. "Big Bob is back in action!"

Bob pumped his fists in the air. *"Yes!"* he shouted. Then he and Jack butted their heads together in a bonding ritual Xander wasn't familiar with. "D'ahh!" Bob grunted as they collided. He grabbed Jack's arms. "I can't believe you raised me! That is so awesome. You are the *coolest!"*

Xander figured this was his best opportunity to make a getaway. "Maybe I should let you guys catch up—"

Jack pointed at Xander with the knife. "Bob, this is Xander," he said. "He's our wheel man."

I have a job description, Xander thought. *Does that mean I'm hired? Because, retiring sounds like a good idea.*

Bob took a step toward Xander, gave him a friendly punch in the shoulder. Didn't quite dislocate it, but it knocked Xander back a couple of steps. "Hey," Bob said.

"Howdy," Xander replied, with a grimace of pain.

"Dude, where are the other guys?" Bob asked Jack. "We gotta go get 'em!"

"Absolutely," Jack agreed.

"All right," Bob said.

Jack started walking toward the car, Bob following.

Xander stayed by the grave. "Are, um . . . are all your friends dead?" he asked. Not really wanting to know the answer.

Jack obliged him by not answering. "Xander, let's roll."

Xander brought up the rear.

"How long I been down?" Bob asked as they walked.

"Eight months. I hadda wait till the stars aligned."

"Oh, eight months! *Man.* I got some catchin' up to do." Bob stopped, jammed a finger into Jack's chest. " 'Walker Texas Ranger.' You been tapin' 'em?"

"Every ep," Jack assured him.

"All right," the zombie said. "We're gonna get the guys together, we're gonna *party,* man." He slapped Xander on the other shoulder. If Xander had any feeling at all left in his arms by the end of this, he'd be happy. "This is gonna be a night to remember," Bob went on. "Yeah!"

"I'm sensing that," Xander agreed quietly.

"The blood of the Earth shall restore him, and he shall rise."

Jack was repeating the same scene at another graveyard. He was, Xander noted, even more efficient with practice.

A horrible head pushed up through the dirt. This one's skin was all discolored, missing in patches, toasty looking, like he'd survived a terrible fire.

Only, without the surviving part.

"Dudes," he said.

And they were off to the next cemetery. As Xander peeled away from the curb with a screech of tires, Bob waved his fists in the air and screamed, "Beeeeer!"

* * *

Giles stood in Restfield Cemetery, a lighted candle in his hand. Torches were lit and jammed into poles before the door of a mausoleum.

Giles spoke the required incantation in Latin. "Do not deny me, spirit guide!" he said. "Let the wisdom of those who have passed be showered upon me!"

Above the mausoleum door, a bright cloud was forming. From within the cloud a deep voice boomed, also speaking Latin.

"These secrets belong to time and the dark regions!" the voice said. "To reveal them would bring Chaos down upon the living Earth!"

"The beast must be fought," Giles insisted. "Our only hope lies in finding its weakness!"

"Seek not! Disturb us no longer!" The cloud blew away on a sudden wind. The torches and candle went out, leaving Giles alone in the dark.

In more ways than one.

Xander saw the end of it. Jack and his pals were repeating their ritual, a few graves over, and he'd wandered this way when he heard Giles's voice. "Giles," he said, relieved to find someone he knew. *And who's alive.* "Hey, what's going on?"

"Oh, I was just trying to gain access to the spirit guides—not going very well, I'm afraid," Giles said. He sounded frustrated as he gathered up the equipment he'd brought with him. "What are you doing here?"

Xander wasn't sure how much he dared to say. It wasn't just that Jack was dangerous and scary. *Although that enters into it.* It was also that he'd been helping Jack, even if somewhat unwittingly. Xander knew how much Giles disapproved of Willow's occasional forays into spellcasting on her own.

Gotta figure raising the dead is even worse, in his book.

"Oh, we were just raising . . . some heck."

Jack's voice called from the other grave site. "Xander! Let's go!"

Xander realized that Giles might be his last chance to leave these zombies behind. If there was a way he could latch onto Giles, without confessing what he'd been up to . . . "Listen, do you guys need any help?"

"Hmm?" Giles asked, distracted by his own worries. "Oh, no. Thank you. Probably best if you stay out of trouble."

"Not much chance of that," Xander said.

Jack and his buddies—including a new one—stood beside the Chevy. "Xander!" Jack yelled. "Motor!"

"There's something different about this menace," Giles went on. "Something in the air. The stench of death."

"Yeah, I think it's Bob," Xander said.

"We may all be called upon to fight when it happens."

Xander was getting a little tired of this "nobody trust Xander with the info" thing. *But maybe Giles isn't in on the conspiracy, he thought. Worth a try* . . . "When what happens, exactly?"

"Come on!" Jack was growing impatient.

And Giles dodged the question. "I'd better go," he said. "Hopefully, we shall have time to prepare. All we need is a few weeks."

"Tonight?" Buffy asked.

"Before sunrise," Willy answered. "That's what they said."

Willy's Alibi Room was completely trashed.

Not that it was particularly stylish in the first place.

Calling it a dive would be kind, Buffy thought. It was the kind of place demons and serious drinkers came to seek oblivion, company, and bruised knuckles. She'd heard about legendary bar brawls that had taken place here, but she was pretty sure that tonight's damage rated pretty high even by Willy's somewhat flexible standards.

Willy himself was a bloody mess, crumpled on the floor behind the bar. His cash register was down there with him, both surrounded by broken bottles. The rest of the place was in the same shape: furniture smashed, mirrors broken, light fixtures torn from the ceiling.

"Why did they do this?" Buffy asked him.

Willy sounded more upset than she had ever heard him. "They were looking for Angel."

"Angel, why?"

"Said they were coming after you, too. Said nothing could stand in their way because tonight was the night." He coughed, clutched his bleeding chest. "Ahh, man."

Buffy was worried about the barkeep. He was a transplanted easterner who had never quite acclimated to southern California. His dark hair and pale skin didn't look like they'd ever seen the sun—not because he was a vampire, but because he worked nights and slept days, she figured.

Willy's wasn't a place she and her friends hung out in—you were supposed to be twenty-one to even get in the door, for one thing. And most of his regulars were demons and other undesirables. Willy always made perfectly clear that his own interests were his number-one priority, and his assistance, when he gave it at all, usually carried a steep price. But she didn't wish him any harm. She'd called 911 as soon as she'd found him. "The ambulance is on its way."

"Look, kid," he said. "My clientele ain't exactly nuns

and orphans. But I never seen anything like these demons."

Coming from him, a statement like that carried some weight. But she wanted to sound confident. "I'm gonna stop them," she promised.

"That Hellmouth opens, they're gonna be the least of your problems, is my train of thought," he said. "If I were you, I'd go find Angel, go somewhere quiet together. I'd be thinking about how I wanna spend my last night on Earth."

The radio was blasting as Xander drove through the normally subdued streets of Sunnydale. Dickie, the burn victim, and Parker, who had been drowned, sat in the back. Both Dickie and Parker, at least, had been buried in the traditional dark suits and ties.

Jack rode shotgun. Bob stood in the middle, between Dickie and Parker, fists raised to the sky.

"Let's get some beer!" he wailed.

Parker had his own ideas. "Let's go pick up some girls, man. We'll hang out Taco Bell, get some girls, go cruise around."

They all laughed at that—but then, Xander noted, they all thought pretty much *everything* was hilarious. *A side effect of being returned from the dead,* he figured.

"I wanna bake a cake," Dickie said, to another round of laughter.

"Hey, we need some beers, though," Bob insisted, taking his seat. The big guy had a one-track mind.

"I can't believe you got shot, man," Parker said. "Was it them Jackals?"

"Are you kidding?" Jack responded. "We wiped them out after they threw you off the bridge."

"Oh, man," Parker said, voice quaking with emotion. "You guys are the best, man. I mean it."

"It was a liquor store," Bob told them. "Little Armenian guy, runs the place, he had a gun behind the counter. Hey, we should go kick his ass!"

"Yeah!" Parker screamed.

"Yeah!" Bob echoed.

Xander couldn't believe he was chauffeuring a bunch of zombie thugs around town. *My folks would have my license if they knew,* he thought. Not to mention what Uncle Rory would do if these guys left some kind of residue, embalming fluid, anything like that, on his pristine seats. "If you guys want me to drop you somewhere, that's—" he began.

"No," Jack said sharply. "You're with us now."

"Yeah, man," Parker agreed. "You're on the team now, baby. Woohoo!"

"What are we gonna do?" Bob asked.

"Well, I've heard some interesting suggestions, but I'm gonna have to go with Dickie's," Jack said. "Let's bake a cake."

This pronouncement was met with a chorus of cheers and catcalls. Xander had to rethink his earlier position. *A bunch of zombie thugs with an interest in the culinary arts.*

He was pretty sure the night couldn't get any weirder.

Jack had Xander pull up outside a hardware store. The gang piled out of the car. "You stay here," Jack said. "And keep the motor running."

"This time of night," Xander suggested, "I'm pretty sure nothing's open—"

Bob threw something through the store's plate-glass window, shattering it. The dead guys pushed their way in through the broken glass.

"Oh," Xander said. "But of *course,* they're always open for crime." He kept his hands on the wheel, eyes in front. He didn't want to see any more of this than he had to.

But he couldn't bring himself to not look.

"Okay, now I'm involved in crime," he said to himself. "I'm the criminal element. Having a car sure is cool."

Across the street, he heard a bell jingle, and a familiar voice.

"Thank you! Sorry to wake you!"

It was Willow! Then he saw her, coming out of a shop doorway. Uncle Bob's Magic Cabinet, the sign over the display window read. There was a man at the door, locking up behind himself. "No problem," the guy said.

Xander got out of the car. "Will!" he called. He felt a wave of relief wash over him—but just as suddenly, it passed.

And you're going to tell her what, exactly? he asked himself. She was his oldest friend; he wasn't going to get her mixed up with the under-the-hill gang. They hadn't been violent yet—toward him, anyway. But it was apparent that they had the capacity.

Willow came across the street toward him. "Xander. What are you doing here?"

"Nothing," he replied. "Certainly not crime!" He glanced back toward the hardware store, making sure the guys weren't coming out yet. "What about you?"

She held up the paper bag she had carried from the shop. "I needed supplies for a protection spell. Buffy called from Angel's. It's happening, tonight."

The mysterious "it." "And that thing that's happening would be . . . ?" he asked.

"I . . . I can't say," Willow stammered. "Buffy'll need this." She started to rush off, then stopped herself. She came back to him, threw her arms around his neck, squeezing him tightly. "I love you, Xander," she said. Then she released him and darted off into the darkness.

Xander watched her go. There was definitely something going on, and he knew he had to be there for Buffy and the others. He had to get away from Jack and his gang. "Okay, that's it" he said. "I'm going to—"

He turned and walked straight into Jack.

"Where you going?"

"Look," Xander said. "Something's just come up."

"You wanna bail on me?" Jack asked quietly. "Is that it?"

Just then, the others came out of the store carrying shopping bags. "We got the cake mix!" Dickie announced.

"Where do you wanna bake it?" Parker asked.

"Xander's looking to leave," Jack told them.

"No *way,*" Bob said. "We need a wheel man."

"Xander doesn't feel he's part of the group," Jack explained. The other guys circled around him.

"No," Xander said. *I don't want to be part of the group.* But he didn't think they'd appreciate hearing that. "I'm kind of busy . . ."

"He doesn't feel like part of the group," Bob said, "because he hasn't been initiated!"

Xander didn't like the sound of that at all. What kind of terrible hazing ritual would these guys come up with? Would he have to break into a store? Kill someone? *No telling.*

"Do you think he's ready?" Jack asked.

"I think he's earned his stripes," Parker said, draping a disfigured arm over Xander's shoulder like a dear friend.

He smelled kind of like a coffeepot that had been left on too long. "I say we let him in, boys."

Outnumbered and surrounded, Xander pasted a big fake smile on his face. "*Great.* I wanna be in the gang, sure."

"All right, yeah!" Parker said.

"That's the spirit," Jack said.

"What do I gotta do?" Xander asked, dreading the answer.

Jack whipped Katie from her sheath, held her up in front of Xander's face. Xander could see himself reflected in the blade. He didn't look happy.

"You gotta die," Jack hissed.

CHAPTER 14

Parker had a firm grip on Xander's collar, and Bob pressed against him from the other side. He wasn't going anywhere.

Jack turned the knife from side to side before Xander's face, as if admiring the way the light played across the expanse of blade.

"All right, guys," Xander said. "Let's just talk about this."

"You wanna be in the gang, don't you?" Parker asked him.

Xander answered nervously. "Yes, but I'm not *dying* to be in the gang. If you get the . . . the pun there."

Bob's sense of humor seemed limited when it came to zombie gags. "What, are you—you're too good to be dead?" he demanded, real anger in his voice for the first time since being raised. He grabbed Xander's jacket in both hammy fists, pulled him up to his own broad, bullet-scarred face. "You got a problem with dead people?"

Xander thought he saw an out. "What about Jack? Jack's not dead."

Wrong.

Jack lifted his T-shirt, revealing a flat stretch of belly marred by multiple bullet holes strung in an uneven line.

Bob released Xander, who looked at the round entry wounds with trepidation.

"Drive by," Jack explained. "Three weeks ago."

"Oh boy," was all Xander could say.

"Grandpappy found my body," Jack went on. "I wasn't gone ten minutes before he raised me. It's a rush, man."

They say skydiving is a rush, too, Xander thought. *And skiing down the slope of Mt. Everest, that's been described as a rush.* Those kinds of rushes, Xander didn't feel any urgency about experiencing.

Same for this one.

"Let's kill Xander!" Dickie urged. "It'll be fun!"

"Yeah, man," Parker agreed. His hand was draped on Xander's shoulder in a friendly way again; he'd relaxed his grip on Xander's collar when Bob had grabbed him. "You could be a full-fledged member."

"Come on, Xander," Jack said. "Take it like a man."

"All right, enough!" Xander insisted. This wasn't going any further. "You guys have had your fun. But you forgot about one thing."

They all stood around, waiting for him to enlighten them.

But there was no "thing." There was only the slimmest hope of catching them off-guard.

Xander bolted.

"Get him!" Jack shouted.

There was a closed coffee shop across the street, the Espresso Pump, with outside tables and chairs behind a low wall. The wall had open sections, blocked at night by chains.

Xander had spent plenty of afternoons at those tables. He knew the layout.

He ducked under one of the chains, racing onto the patio area. The zombies came in on two sides, under the chains, and as they did Xander leapt to one of the tables, then back over the wall.

Fortunately, he had, as Jack had instructed, left the engine running in the Bel Air.

As the guys came back out from the patio, Xander jumped into the car, slammed it into gear, and peeled off down the street.

They watched the car turn a corner, and it was gone. No way to chase it on foot.

"Damn!" Bob said, furious. "There goes the wheels."

"He took all our stuff, man," Parker said.

One-track Dickie added, "I wanna bake a cake!"

"It's all right. We'll get more," Jack said. The voice of reason. "The night is young."

They headed back into the hardware store.

Blocks away, Xander was still breathing hard. He could feel his heart hammering in his chest and throat and temples. There wasn't anything about the feeling he liked, except for the fact that his heart hadn't been cut out of his chest.

"I'd say that's pretty much enough excitement for one evening," he said to himself as he gunned the engine. The more miles between him and the "boys," the better.

He didn't even slow down for the corners. The streets were empty. He screeched around one, headed for the park.

And spotted Faith, locked in mortal struggle with one of those grotesque blue-skinned lady demons like the ones they'd fought a couple of nights before.

Well, that the others fought, while I hid. But still . . .

Buffy and Faith had said they were tough customers, even then, when the whole gang was allied against them. This one was taking on Faith all by herself, and seemed to have the edge.

As Xander pulled out of the turn, the demon had Faith up against a wire fence. Faith got two handfuls of fence and kicked out with both feet, and the demon was knocked several steps backward.

Into the parking lot.

Xander floored it.

The demon made a satisfying thudding sound as the front end of the big Chevy plowed into her. She was thrown back into the grass.

Xander backed up, jerked to a stop.

"Get in!" he shouted.

Faith got in.

The demon was already regaining her feet.

Xander threw the car into gear and raced back out into the street.

They weren't going to beat that demon tonight. But it couldn't outrun them.

Having a car sure is cool, Xander thought. This time, he meant it.

Faith had a room at the Downtowner Motel. She hadn't been in town long enough to find permanent digs, but she'd already proven herself a loyal and helpful ally to Buffy. Even though she wasn't strictly needed, since one Slayer was usually traditional, it never hurt to have two.

Xander pulled into the motel parking lot, cranked the car into a slot in front of Room 3. They dashed from the car into the room, locking the door behind them. Xander peeked out through the window blinds.

"You think Demon Mama followed us?" he asked.

"Naw," Faith said. She stripped off her jacket. Beneath it she wore a tight black tank top. "We're cool." She winced. "The bitch dislocated my shoulder, though. Hold me."

Xander wasn't quite sure how she meant that. Sure, she was a beautiful girl, and she looked great in that skimpy top and tight pants. But they'd never been alone like this before, in a motel room. *Could she . . . ?*

He went to her, arms out to give her a hug.

And she breathed a little annoyed huff, took his hand, positioned it on her shoulder. She pressed her own hand against his chest, and wrenched her shoulder back into place.

The sound was like snapping a branch. Xander cringed.

But at least I know where we stand, he thought.

"That's better," Faith said.

But, oddly, she didn't take her hand away from his chest. Instead, she began moving it, gently, in ever widening circles.

"She really got me wound up," Faith said. "A fight like that and no kill, I'm about ready to pop."

"Really?" Xander asked, swallowing hard. "Pop?"

By which she means . . . ?

Her left hand came up behind his head, stroking the back of his neck. "You up for it?" she asked.

And her right hand dropped lower, deft fingers unbuttoning his shirt as it went.

"Oh, I'm up," he agreed. "I'm suddenly very up."

She moved closer to him. Her lips were parted, and he could feel her breath, hot on his chest. She smelled good. Like sweat, but also like soap and shampoo and, well, *female.*

He felt the need to clarify his meaning . . . *or is it just the need to babble senselessly?* "It's just that I've never been up with people, before."

She pressed her lips against his, shutting off any further conversation for a moment.

He liked it.

A lot.

She broke the kiss. "Just relax," she breathed. "And take your pants off."

"Those two concepts are antithetical," he pointed out.

She kissed him again, a kiss that gave him the willingness to try to overlook any apparent contradictions.

She yanked his shirt and jacket down off his shoulders, throwing them to the floor. Kissed him again, hard and long.

She spun him around and hurled him to the bed.

As he watched, spellbound, she climbed on top, straddling him, and peeled her own shirt off.

"Don't worry," she said. "I'll steer you 'round the curves."

He wondered, briefly, why he'd never come up with this car angle before. "Did I mention that I'm having a very strange night?" he asked.

Then there was no more talking for a while.

Afterwards, she led him to the door, opened it. He stepped outside, shirt, jacket, and shoes in his hands.

She had, at least, given him time to pull his pants on.

"That was great," Faith said. "I gotta shower."

She shut the door, locking it behind her. Apparently she hadn't been thinking long-term commitment.

Or even, short-term conversation. Didn't girls like to talk after? Go out for bagels? Make wedding plans? *Or is that all a myth perpetuated by the more experienced to scare the rest of us away from joining the club?*

Bright side, at least I've still got the car.

Inside the book cage, Oz snarled and growled, leaping against the door.

"I've never seen him like this," Willow said, worried about her friend.

"It's the Hellmouth," Giles explained. "He can sense it's going to open." He handed Willow the tranquilizer rifle. "Be ready just in case."

Giles went to the cage door, shoved his key into the lock.

"Now, don't hesitate," he said as he turned it.

Willow raised the gun to her shoulder, sighted down its length. "Do it."

"Now Oz—" Giles began. He opened the door.

And Oz slammed into it, driving Giles back into the wall. The werewolf took a single step into the library and Willow pulled the trigger. The tranquilizer dart flew into Oz, its impact knocking his legs out from under him. He hit the floor with a wail of pain.

But he was on his feet again in less than a second, and coming for Willow.

"Again!" Giles cried.

Willow tried to shove another dart into place. Her fingers fumbled. She backed up as Oz leapt to the top of the table in front of her. He was ready to pounce.

He'd kill her in a flash.

Giles came up behind him, throwing his strong arms around Oz's wolfen form, and restrained him.

He couldn't hold Oz for long, though.

Finally, the dart slid home. She lifted the weapon, aimed, fired.

Oz went limp in Giles's arms. The librarian put him down on the table.

"We've got to move him before he wakes up," Giles said.

Willow knew he was right. If the Hellmouth opened, there wouldn't be any good places to be—but locked up here would be the worst place possible.

She stroked his fur. "Sorry," she said. "I hope you're not mad at me in the morning."

Xander was confused. He tugged on his clothes in the parking lot, standing next to his car. She'd thrown him out the door. It was nothing but a physical release, for her.

But at the same time, he felt great. Fantastic. Triumphant, even.

Okay, maybe she had done more conquering than he, in this instance. But still . . .

He felt great.

He opened the door, got into the car.

Looked at himself in the rearview mirror. He didn't *look* any different.

But he was different, and he knew it.

Everything changes.

Then, in the rearview, he caught a glimpse of Dickie's "ingredients," still in the backseat. He reached back, got the bag, brought it up front with him. Rustled through it.

A big can of kerosene. A coiled length of wire. A nine-volt battery. An alarm clock.

"Hey," Xander said to himself. "They're not baking any cake."

He drove back to the hardware store. The street was empty. The smashed out window gave silent testimony to the fact that the zombies had been here, but otherwise there was no sign of them.

"Long gone," he said. "Probably loaded with supplies. Gotta think."

He thought for a moment. "I can't believe I had sex." *Wrong, Xander. No time for that.* "Okay, bombs," he said. "Already dead guys with bombs. Oh, man, I'm out of my league." He pounded on the door with his fist. "Buffy'll know what to do," he said. He stepped on the gas.

"I don't know what to do," Buffy said.

She and Angel were in the garden of his mansion. She'd taken Willy's advice, after all. Find Angel, he had said.

Not surprisingly, Angel had also been looking for her. He had a knack for knowing when he was really needed.

Tonight, he's really needed.

They were lit by candles. A fire flickered nearby.

Any other time, Buffy thought, *this would all be devastatingly romantic.*

"Then let me decide for you," Angel said grimly. "I can face this thing."

"You can't!"

"Look," he argued. "I can at least buy you enough time for Willow's spell to bind it. Buffy, this is worse than anything we've ever faced. Honey, it's the only way."

She was afraid that he was right. But he couldn't be. She wouldn't let him be.

Angel was the only man—if the definition of "man" could be stretched a little—she'd ever loved. And they'd been parted too many times.

"I can't watch you die again," she told him.

He stroked her cheek with the backs of his fingers, tenderly. "I love you."

She raised a hand to his, held it against her face.

"I love you," Buffy said.

"Nothing can change that," Angel assured her. "Not even death."

She threw his hand away from her, backed away from him.

"Don't talk to me like that!" she said angrily. "You may be ready to go but I am not ready to lose you. Okay, this is my fight and if you won't do it my way then you—"

Xander cleared his throat. He stood in the garden entryway, feeling bad for interrupting what seemed to be a very heartfelt discussion. But he didn't know where else to turn.

They both whirled to face him. He felt suddenly like he was under a spotlight.

Not the most pleasant feeling.

"Hey, I've got this . . ." he stammered. "Um . . . there's this, uh . . . it's probably a bad time."

From the expressions on their faces, he knew he was right.

"Can I help?" he asked.

Buffy gave the slightest shake of her head.

"Okay," Xander said. He left them to their argument, and went up the garden stairs toward the street.

"I gotta work this out," he said as he climbed. "I just gotta figure out what they'd be likely to bomb."

Giles intoned the recitation in the appropriate Latin.

"Earth, wind, fire, and rain. All four powers I beseech you. Protect us from fresh evil unleashed . . ."

As he spoke, he moved around a mystical circle painted on the library floor, lighting candles with a long one he held in his hand.

Willow interrupted, coming breathlessly into the library.

"Okay," she said, as Giles continued with his candle-lighting. "Oz is moved. He could barely walk after that mickey I gave him, but we made it." She put the tranquilizer rifle down on the counter. "Is he gonna be all right there?"

"Anywhere is safer than here," Giles assured her. He tossed her an unlit candle. "Help me with the candles."

"We're doing the binding spell from the *Hebron's Almanac?*" Willow asked.

"Yes, but once it's ready, you're to stay back and let me finish the recitation," Giles replied. She started to say something, but he cut her off. "Don't argue. I want you safe. Who knows what's going to come up from beneath us?"

Willow knelt to light her candle from an already glowing one on the floor.

And beneath the library, four forms moved in the school's boiler room. Dickie worked inside a bizarre configuration of wires and pipes. Attached to it all was a digital alarm clock.

As Dickie connected two wires, the alarm clock flashed 9:55. Then, a moment later, the display beeped and changed to read 60:00. The red numbers were bright in the dim room.

Dickie laughed.

The display changed again, to 59:59, and began to beep down through the seconds. 59:58. 59:57.

"This is gonna be large," Jack said.

"Oh, yeah," Dickie agreed.

He did love to bake.

CHAPTER 15

Agitated, Xander drummed on the wheel with his thumbs as he drove the dark streets. *Where to turn . . . ?*

"Giles'll know what to do," he said. "He's way more calm than Buffy."

And Giles could usually be found at the school library. Unless something big was brewing.

Like tonight.

Xander realized he had no idea where to look for Giles. He'd start with the library anyway. Then, if that didn't pan out—

He came around a corner. There were four guys walking down the middle of the street, ahead of him. Going the same direction he was going.

Four dead guys.

The boys.

"Okay," he said to himself. "I need a plan." *And I need it now.*

As he pulled up behind them, he slowed down.

"Hey," Bob said. "Our wheels!"

They parted as he drove between them, cruising at about the speed they'd been walking. Letting them think, Xander hoped, that he was going to allow them back into the car.

They laughed.

Xander reached over the door, grabbed Parker's arm.

Gunned it.

"Hey!" He heard behind him. He kept going, through another turn. Leaving them behind.

Except Parker, who gripped his hand. His dead, crispy face was contorted in fear. Parker's feet scrabbled along the road as the car raced away.

"Stop!" Parker screamed. "Come on, man, stop!"

But Xander kept going. His plan was working. It was a spur of the moment thing, a last-ditch attempt at a plan. *But so far, so good.* "Where's the bomb?" he asked.

Parker didn't even hesitate. "It's in the high school!"

Xander fought to control the big car with his right hand. It weaved from side to side. If there had been any traffic they'd have *both* been dead.

"In the school where?" he demanded.

"This really really hurts!" Parker all but cried. *So the dead can feel pain,* Xander observed. *Good to know.* "It's in the—in the boiler room!"

Xander struggled to keep the car going straight. Looking into Parker's eyes instead of the road, he used his best tough-guy voice.

"All right," he said. "Now I'm gonna ask you this once, and you better pray you get the answer right. How do I defuse—"

But he had veered too far to the left, and a jutting mailbox collided with Parker's head.

The mailbox stayed where it was.

Parker's head stayed with it.

Xander was holding a headless corpse in his left hand.

He yelped and let go.

"I probably should've left out that whole middle part," he said. He made a left, and headed toward Sunnydale High School.

Behind him, the other three ran full out. "He's heading for the school!" Dickie called.

"That's it!" Jack replied. He'd had enough of this kid.

Xander was going to pay.

Xander burst into the school at a dead run. He almost passed the door that said "Basement Access: Door to Remain Locked at All Times," but he backtracked to it, gripped the knob.

Locked.

Sometimes you just had to believe the signs.

And through the same outside door he'd just entered came Jack, Dickie, and Bob. "There he is!" Jack shouted.

"Where's a Slayer when you need one?" Xander asked, taking off.

Buffy stood in the library. Ranked around her were Angel, Willow, Giles, and Faith.

They looked on in awe and horror.

The beast was huge and terrible. Multiple heads snapped and growled on long, stalk-like necks. Tentacles waved in the air. The thing was nearly as tall as the library's high ceiling.

Mystical lightning flared in the room, the only illumination.

It had come from the Hellmouth. What terrified Buffy was the idea that there might be more, or worse, still to come.

The only one holding a weapon of any kind was Willow, who gripped a spike-headed medieval mace.

"My God . . . it's grown . . ." Giles said.

Her Watcher's fear frightened Buffy all the more.

Dickie stopped outside the library, drawn by the strobes of light showing through the door's round windows. He looked inside. Five people were staring at a monster the likes of which he had never imagined. Even dying hadn't held such terror.

"Wow!"

But Jack was still on Xander's trail. "Come on, man!" he shouted. Dickie followed.

They came through double swinging doors into an intersection. No Xander in sight.

"Which way?" Bob asked.

"He couldn't have gotten far," Jack said. "Let's split up."

They did, each taking a different arm of the hallway.

Bob descended a staircase. Hung on the wall, behind a glass panel, was a fire ax. He drove a big fist through the glass, yanked the ax from its tethers, looked at the sharp blade.

"Good for chopping," he noted.

Xander ran into the darkened student lounge, dodging tables and chairs as he went. He had to find a way to the boiler room, and he had to do it fast. *Funny how a guy can spend four years in a place and still not know how to get to something as significant as, say, a boiler room, when he needs it,* he thought. *Who knows when you might have to boil something?* He raced up the two steps into the elevated seating area.

But a form rose up out of the dark. Big Bob. Carrying something that whistled when he swung it.

Xander backstepped away from the swinging ax. His foot missed the step behind him and he went down. At the bottom of the stairs he hit a table, upended it. He landed on the floor, winded.

He tried to scramble to his feet, but Bob was there. He swung the butt end of the ax handle into Xander's jaw. Xander saw a bright flash—*not stars, like in the cartoons, but close*—and fell again, back pressed against one of the tables.

Bob raised the ax over his head.

"Now this is what I call fun," he said.

He swung.

Only one chance.

Xander rolled off the table, just before the ax fell. Its blade bit into the tabletop, stuck there. As Bob struggled to free it, Xander punched him in the face, then grabbed his letter jacket and slammed him down against the tabletop, hard. Dazed, Bob dropped to the floor.

Xander yanked the ax free of the table. He stood, for just a moment, with the weapon in his hands. Looking at Bob on the floor, an easy target.

One swing.

And hey, he's already dead. What do I have to lose?

But he couldn't bring himself to do it. Chopping an unconscious victim—even a walking dead one—just seemed *wrong* somehow.

Besides, he's already dead—what if he just gets up and comes after me, anyway? Beheading him might just make him mad.

In this case, trapping might be more efficient. Xander crossed to a soda machine, standing next to the wall. He shoved the ax handle behind the machine, for leverage, and pushed. The machine swayed. Xander grunted, pushed harder.

The soda machine toppled forward.

With a wet thump, Bob disappeared beneath it.

Dickie came into the lounge, drawn by the noise.

He saw the machine, saw Bob's legs sticking out from underneath.

Xander stepped from the shadows, fire ax in his hands.

Forget the "talk softly, big stick" bit, he told himself. *Talk tough, and carry a big ax. Much better advice.*

"Shoulda learned by now," Xander said. "If you're gonna play with fire, you got to expect that sooner or later—"

Dickie ran, back out the door through which he'd entered.

"I wasn't finished!" Xander yelled at his departing form.

He gave chase. As he ran, he said, "Note to self: less talk."

Buffy sailed backward through the library doors, blowing them open. She landed twenty feet away, on the hard tile floor. Tentacles twitched and quivered in the doorway. Smoke poured from the room.

This isn't going at all well, she thought.

She pushed herself to her feet, shaking her head. Gathering her courage.

The creature was too strong. It was going to be hard to go back in there.

But it was also necessary. She was the Slayer. She did what she had to do.

"Faith!" she called as she headed back into the fray. At least she wasn't, currently, the only Slayer. "Go for the heart!"

Xander was right on Dickie's heels. Still carrying the ax. Dickie made a couple of sharp turns, going down a narrow hallway. Xander right behind.

A moment later, Xander came back out of the hallway, running even faster. Behind him, Dickie was turning up the juice.

Behind Dickie, three she-demons. The ugly blue-gray ones, all horns and teeth.

What was it Bob had said? "A night to remember?" Isn't that also the name of a movie about the Titanic?

Encouraging thought, Harris.

Xander made a quick right and ducked into a patch of shadow. Dickie missed the turn, though, and ran straight into a classroom.

Classrooms only had one door.

The demons followed him in there. Xander heard snarling and spitting, and saw Dickie pressed up against the blinds over the window in the room's door.

Dickie screamed. Bad as that sound was, it wasn't quite as bad as the sounds of biting and chewing that accompanied it. The demons weren't much on table manners.

Two down, Xander thought.

He took a deep breath. "Okay, boiler room—"

He began to head for it, but before he'd gone more than a step the wall exploded in front of him. A huge, eyeless head—eyeless, but not mouthless or toothless—burst through the plaster, at the end of a thick snake-like neck. It sensed him, turned toward him. *I hate to be insensitive,* Xander thought, *but you're Buffy's problem. I have worries of my own.*

"—other way," he said.

He ran.

The ax, it turned out, made it easy to unlock the basement access door. Xander clomped down the stairs, ax ready just in case.

He opened the door into the boiler room. It was narrow, filled with strange-looking mechanical equipment. The boiler, Xander presumed. There was another door, with an illuminated exit sign, across from him. On that door was a sign that said "Keep Door Closed at All Times."

Which makes you wonder why it's a door at all then, he thought. *If you just had a wall there you could save yourself the trouble of making the sign.*

The bomb was in the center of the room, right where Parker had promised just before being decapitated by the U.S. Mail. It sat atop a dark green fifty-gallon metal drum.

"Hello, nasty," Xander said to it. He closed the door behind him. Examined the bomb.

Which, of course, he knew nothing about. He was capable of reading a digital clock, though. "Less than two minutes," he said. "Dumb guy. Little bomb. How hard can it be?"

Something hit him on the back of the head. He blinked with the force, then felt himself being hurled against a tool cabinet.

Ribs aching, head throbbing, he pulled himself to his feet.

Jack O'Toole stood there, breathing hard.

"It just got harder," Jack said.

"I'm not leaving here until that thing is disarmed," Xander vowed.

"Then I guess you're not leaving."

Jack swung at Xander. Xander dodged. Jack came at him again, fists flying. Xander took a couple of hits. On top of all the other punishment he'd taken today, though, he barely felt them.

But then Jack had him up against a wall. He whisked Katie from her home, brought her toward Xander. Xander caught Jack's arm, trying to hold it back. The knife hovered an inch from Xander's face.

Getting really tired of that knife, Xander thought. *Maybe if Jack dated girls more, he wouldn't feel so attached to Katie.*

"I'm gonna carve you up and serve you with gravy," Jack threatened. "You piss me off, boy, now you pay the price. First the eyes, then the tongue, then I'll break every one of your fingers—"

"You gonna do all that in forty-nine seconds?" Xander asked through clenched teeth.

Jack turned to look at the clock. Xander jerked himself free, slammed his fists into Jack's midsection. When Jack doubled over, Xander drove him into a wall.

Jack came back fighting. He punched at Xander, missed, but caught Xander's jacket. He flipped Xander over and threw him to the floor.

Xander regained his footing. He stood between Jack and both doors.

They faced each other, Jack's gaze darting between the bomb and the exit sign and the door to the stairwell Xander had come down.

"I know what you're thinking," Xander said, panting.

"Can I get by him? Get up the stairs, out of the building? Seconds ticking away. I don't love your chances."

"Then you'll die too," Jack rasped.

"Yeah, looks like," Xander agreed. "So I guess the question really is . . . who has less fear?"

"I'm not afraid to die," Jack reminded him. "I'm already dead."

Xander wasn't buying. "Yeah, but this is different. Being blown up isn't 'walking around and drinking with your buddies' dead. It's 'little bits swept up by a janitor' dead, and I don't think you're ready for that."

Jack's breathing was ragged. He looked at the bomb. At the door. Made a feint toward one door.

Xander moved, so he stayed between Jack and the way out.

Any way out.

The clock beeped off the seconds.

"Are you?" Jack asked.

Xander smiled, suddenly more calm than he had any reason to be. He knew the answer. He'd spent the last few years telling his friends he wasn't afraid, that he was willing to help battle whatever the Hellmouth threw at them. Swallowing his fear, pretending courage when he felt none.

Tonight had been a lifetime. Everything had happened to him, and he was still standing.

He wasn't bluffing anymore. "I like the quiet," was all he said.

The battle in the library raged. Members of the Sisterhood of Jhe had joined the Hellmouth creature. Weapons were wielded—swords, axes, Willow's mace. But the creature wasn't phased.

It had Buffy wrapped in a tentacle, holding her off the

floor, almost up to the ceiling. She gripped an ax tightly in her fists.

Giles was speaking in Latin, screaming to be heard above the roar, slashing at the thing as he did so. ". . . and all the vessels of truth!" The ritual words finished, he shouted, "Now, Buffy!"

Overhead, she slammed her ax down into the tentacle that held her, again and again, feeling it bite into hellish flesh and sinew. Hot blood splashed her hands and arms.

Xander waited. He felt centered, at peace.

The clock beeped. Seconds flashed by in red crystal digits.

00:12.

00:11.

Jack was a wreck. Twitching, nervous gaze darting around the room.

00:05.

00:04.

Jack reached into the mechanism, grabbed a wire. Tugged on it.

00:02.

The clock went dark.

When the building didn't blow up, Xander said, "Good boy." His calm was suddenly gone, as he realized what he had risked. He walked around to stand beside Jack. His voice trembled a little when he spoke, but still, he spoke with authority. "I don't think I wanna be seeing you on campus anymore, Jack."

Jack didn't answer.

Xander kept his legs from turning to jelly and left him there, with the useless collection of parts that had once been a bomb. He went through the door he had come in, back up the stairs toward the school.

When Xander was gone, Jack said, "I'm not going anywhere, Harris." He crossed to the other door, ignoring the Keep Door Closed at All Times sign. He turned the knob, pulled it open. "And the first time you turn your back—"

Oz leapt through the door with a ferocious roar.

Jack screamed.

EPILOGUE

They spoke quietly, sitting at a picnic table on campus. They were out of the sun, in the shade of a spreading tree, and the day was cool.

But beautiful.

Giles's left hand was bandaged, and the left side of his face torn, gashed by unearthly claws. His right eye was blackened, the bruise reaching all the way back to his temple. Buffy's right arm was wrapped in a bright blue sling. A butterfly bandage over Willow's right eye held her eyebrow together.

Their wounds were nothing.

"Even after the Hellmouth was closed," Willow observed, "you could hear it screaming."

"But Angel's gonna be okay?" Oz asked.

"He was only out for a few minutes," Buffy replied. "Longest of my life."

"I'll never forget that thing's face. Its real face, I mean," Willow said quietly.

"Yes," Giles agreed.

Buffy looked at the man she would always consider to be her Watcher. *No matter what the Watchers' Council thinks.* "I don't know how you managed . . . it was the bravest thing I've ever seen."

"The stupidest." Giles smiled, embarrassed. "But the world continues to turn."

"No one will ever know how close it came to stopping," Willow said, looking around her. "Never know what we did."

Which is, Buffy thought, *the way it's supposed to be.*

Xander saw his best friends sitting together, approached the table. He still hadn't told anyone about last night. The bomb, the boiler room, the zombie gang. They'd had problems of their own, he knew. "Guys," he said.

They all looked up at him.

"Xander," Willow said. "Boy, you're lucky you weren't at school last night. It was crazed."

Maybe he wouldn't tell. Driving around afterward, he'd come to some conclusions. One of which was that he could hold his own, no matter what anyone believed. And the other, more significant one, was that it really didn't matter *what* anyone else thought. What was important was knowing his own capabilities, his own depths.

So he swallowed it. He wouldn't say anything. "Well, uh, give me the quiet life," he said. "I'm gonna grab a snack. Anyone want?"

Giles, Buffy, and Willow shook their heads. Oz just stared down at the picnic table.

"Oz?" Xander asked.

Oz looked at him. "No," he said finally. "I'm oddly full today."

" 'kay," Xander said. He walked away from the table, a half-smile playing across his lips.

He felt good. He felt confident. The smile grew.

And here came Cordelia.

"Oh, look, it's mister excitement," she said. "On another life or death doughnut mission? Or are we cruising for bimbos again? Giving them lessons in lack of cool."

Xander kept the smile. And, he realized, the confidence. He just looked at her.

Smiling.

"What?" she asked.

He said nothing. He knew the smile said it all.

"What?" she repeated. Her voice had more of an edge to it this time.

He walked away. Taking in a deep breath. An all-is-right-with-the-world breath.

Smiling.

"*What?*" Cordelia demanded again, behind him.

She was hating this.

He was loving it.

Smiling.

About the Author

Jeff Mariotte is a co-owner of the specialty bookstore Mysterious Galaxy, senior editor for the comic book publisher WildStorm Productions/DC Comics, and writer of many comic books, including the series Desperadoes, and the occasional novel. He's currently working on *Buffy the Vampire Slayer: The Watcher's Guide, Vol. 2* with Nancy Holder and Maryelizabeth Hart. His next novel will be *Gen13: Time and Chance,* cowritten with Scott Ciencin. He lives in San Diego with his rapidly growing family and some animals. He's way too busy.

ABOUT THE AUTHOR

Jeff Mariotte is the co-owner of the specialty bookstore Mysterious Galaxy, senior editor for the comic book publisher WildStorm Productions/DC Comics, and writer of many comic books, including the series Desperadoes, and the occasional novel. He's currently working on *Buffy the Vampire Slayer: The Watcher's Guide, Vol. 2* with Nancy Holder and Maryelizabeth Hart. His next novel will be *Gen13: Time and Chance*, cowritten with Scott Ciencin. He lives in San Diego with his rapidly growing family and some animals. He's way too busy.